AF254681

DESTINY AUTHORS

Award-winning screenplay

by

ESRA ÇENGEL

esrinart

Copyright © 2025 Esra Çengel
All rights reserved.

BEST SCREENPLAY
Bridge Fest, Canada

BEST SCREENPLAY
The Gladiator Film Festival, Türkiye

BEST SCREENPLAY
Tabriz Cinema Awards, Iran

BEST SCREENPLAY
Golden Wheat Awards, Türkiye

BEST SCREENPLAY
Rohip International Film Festival, India

BEST SCREENPLAY
Andromeda Film Festival, Türkiye

BEST SCREENPLAY
Kiev International Film Festival, Ukraine

RUNNER-UP
Jaipur International Film Festival, India

HONORABLE MENTION
Bridge Fest, Canada

QUARTER-FINALIST
Mediterranean Film Festival, Italy

OFFICIAL SELECTION
The Buddha International Film Festival, India

OFFICIAL SELECTION
Universe Multicultural Film Festival, USA

OFFICIAL SELECTION
Great Message International Film Festival, India

FOREWORD;

The indescribable beauty of the Earth is only one of the wonderful gifts that have been given to us, and yet we are the ones who destroy that gift through greed and egoism. We never hesitate to harm the world's blessings, as we want to get a larger share of them. This must be the ultimate irony on this planet.

I believe that life is the most challenging and also the most fun game on Earth. I believe that the consequences of our thoughts and actions are stalking us at all times. I believe that even seemingly minor decisions can have major impacts on our lives. I believe it is always there, as long as we truly desire to see the magical glitter within us. Each of us may have unique individual purposes in life, yet I believe that our common purpose is to contribute to the collective consciousness of humanity in a positive way.

"Destiny Authors" was written for people who feel lost and constantly wonder why their lives keep going off track. I wish to pique the interest of those who haven't discovered the divine power within them yet, as well as remind those who have long forgotten about it.

LOGLINE;

A young woman makes a seemingly minor mistake that creates a ripple effect and inadvertently causes the deaths of all four members of a robbery gang, all while she falls in love with one of them in the parallel universe without knowing he is a criminal.

DESTINY AUTHORS

FADE IN:

EXT. STREETS, LONDON – DAY

Birds fly around Westminster Abbey. The clock reads 8:08 a.m. People jog, avoiding snow puddles. Traffic flows on wet streets. The city becomes shady when the morning sun hides behind a scudding cloud.

A speedy YELLOWISH JALOPY splatters mud on a HUNCHBACK OLD LADY, 75.

Two GLAZIERS in their thirties, one TALL and one SHORT, transfer a piece of cut window glass to the delivery car.

A GARBAGE TRUCK pulls up near a waste container.

The TV ZAP SOUND in the background is interrupted by the NEWSREADER's voice.

> NEWSREADER#1 (V.O.)
> Good morning from a windy Sunday,
> and welcome to the Weekend News! As
> many of you might remember, thousands
> of people protested the sharp hike in
> fuel prices last Wednesday. Opposition
> activists took to the streets, raising
> slogans and clashing with security forces.

A teen boy, ELLIOT, 15, rides his bicycle towards the pigeons by the sidewalk to scare them, but he loses his balance and falls into a mud puddle. The water bottle in the bike basket rolls down the sidewalk.

INT. AUTO REPAIR SHOP – DAY

DANIEL, 50, a master mechanic, works on a pink old car. An APPRENTICE MECHANIC, 25, struggles with the gray one.

Elliot in his muddy clothes enters, dragging his bicycle. His father Daniel angrily throws the bicycle into the storeroom and locks its door, while Elliot bashfully washes off his bruised hands.

                NEWSREADER#1 (V.O.)(CON'T)
          Several injured people and a number of
          damaged store windows were reported
          at the scene, and twenty-four people
          have been taken into custody by now.

INT. FLOOR#2, OLIVER'S BUILDING – DAY

A modest apartment building. A REDHEAD, 30, walks up the stairs with her LITTLE SON, 5, who is eating a muffin. They are unaware that a piece of muffin fell in the hallway.

                NEWSREADER#1 (V.O.)(CON'T)
          On the other hand, a statement was
          released by the authorities.

INT. KITCHEN, VIOLET'S APARTMENT – DAY

A pretty girl in a mini nightgown, VIOLET, 22, places an avocado sandwich on an old sandwich maker and secures the clasp. The newscast is on the air on a small TV.

                NEWSREADER#1 (O.S.)(CON'T)
          According to the press release, the
          renewed fuel prices might help to
          smooth the traffic flow in the city.

Violet shakes her head in disbelief and switches the channel. She puts some dog food in a bowl and summons the pet dog.

                    VIOLET
          Destiny! Come here, sweetie, it's
          breakfast time!

The dog rushes into the kitchen and eats its food. Violet pours plenty of almond milk into her bowl of cereal.

                    NEWSREADER#2 (O.S.)
        ...The mobile store robbery that occurred
        on Friday morning is still being investigated
        by police. They are seeking for the suspects
        who have vanished with more than seventy
        smartphones and--

Violet switches the channel again, eating her cereal.

                    NEWSREADER#3 (O.S.)
        ... Tomorrow will be a tough day for the
        once-famous actress known as The Wingless
        Fairy, who is accused of murdering her
        husband on New Year's Eve. Her mother-
        in-law has asserted that the life insurance
        was the reason for this brutal and also--

                    VIOLET
        Shoot, it's all about money!

Violet finally turns the TV off. When she leans forward to grab her
sociology book, her long hair dips into the cereal bowl. She heads for
the bathroom to clean the milk from her hair.

INT. KITCHEN, OLIVER'S APARTMENT – DAY

A positive-looking young man, OLIVER, 32, turns on the coffee maker
while talking on his cellphone.

                    OLIVER
        No, babe, no. If you won't honor my
        breakfast table, then I won't be eating
        the whole day. No, no, let's say the
        whole week. What emotional blackmail?
        No, it's not.

Oliver CHUCKLES while washing one of the dirty mugs in the sink. His
smile then fades somehow.

                    OLIVER (CON'T)
          Yeah, right, you'll have that biggy meeting
          tomorrow. The one with the shareholders,
          right? God, those Italian guys are really
          jangling my nerves. "Why?" Do you think
          jealousy is unique to you?

Oliver opens the fridge. There is one green apple and some leftover pizza. Oliver grabs the apple, thinks short, the puts it back and closes the fridge. He grabs the peanut butter jar from the shelf.

                    OLIVER (CON'T)
          Okay, babe, I give up, but at least don't
          ignore my dad's dinner invitation for
          tonight. He'll make his special fish
          recipe for us. You know he'll get more
          upset than me if you don't show up.

INT. LIVING ROOM, JESSICA'S APARTMENT – DAY

A neat, lilac-furnished room. A mirrored dresser displays an engagement photo of "Oliver and Jessica" in a vintage frame, as well as two keys attached to a large letter "O."

JESSICA, 30, a beautiful young woman in a lovely dress, applies lipstick while talking on her cellphone.

                    JESSICA
          Of course, I'll be there. Would I ever
          upset him? Oh, give me a break, honey.
          You know that I'd never upset you, either.
          Well, at least, not until the day you hurt me.

INTERCUT WITH OLIVER IN HIS KITCHEN:

Oliver responds to Jessica confidently:

                    OLIVER
          There is no such day on my calendar,
          babe!

The coffee maker suddenly BEEPS with a FLASHING RED LIGHT. Oliver turns it off to figure out the problem.

> OLIVER (CON'T)
> No, it's just the coffee maker. Pissed
> off because you ditched us this morning.
> Okay, you keep resting, babe. I'll pick
> you up around six. Yeah, and I'll keep
> painting. Love you, too, babe.

Oliver restarts the coffee maker. He ignores its strange noise as long as it's brewing. He takes off his sweatshirt and flips through an auto magazine. He dips into the jar and sucks on his peanut-buttered fingers.

INT. LIVING ROOM, JESSICA'S APARTMENT – DAY

Jessica delicately places a lilac envelope and a lilac handkerchief into her purse. She studies herself in the mirror and inhales deeply, as if she needs to boost her courage. She grabs her purse and leaves the apartment.

INT. KITCHEN, VIOLET'S APARTMENT – DAY

The dog licks the last crumbs in its bowl. Violet enters, tying her half-wet hair into a ponytail. She sees the SMOKE RISING from the sandwich maker. She panics even more when the smoke detector loudly CHIRPS with a FLASHING RED LIGHT.

> VIOLET
> Oh, shoot!

Violet unplugs the sandwich maker and opens the window. She swings a hand towel around to get rid of the smoke.

> VIOLET (CON'T)
> Airflow! I need airflow!

She rushes towards the apartment door, unaware of the dog tagging along.

INT. FLOOR#2, OLIVER'S BUILDING - DAY

Just as Violet opens the door, the dog flees towards the muffin piece in the hallway. Violet lunges reflexively.

> VIOLET
> Destiny, where are you headed?

The BANGING of the kitchen window is HEARD. The door SLAMS SHUT because of the strong airflow. Violet is locked out. The dog runs upstairs after swallowing the muffin piece.

INT. LIVING ROOM, OLIVER'S APARTMENT – DAY

A brand-new coffee table and a sofa are still wrapped in plastic. The song "TOO MUCH" is played on a vintage record player. Oliver aversely paints the walls lilac while singing along with "Billy Fury."

> OLIVER
> "Don't leave me with a broken heart,
> cause I love you too much!"

The DOORBELL RINGS. Oliver quickly throws the dirty socks and shirts behind the sofa.

> OLIVER
> I knew you were on the way to me, babe!

INT. FOYER, OLIVER'S APARTMENT – DAY

Oliver is stumped just as he opens the apartment door. Violet, with a ponytail, is standing at his door with the dog in her arms.

> VIOLET
> (timidly)
> Morning...

> OLIVER
> Hi...?

Oliver sees a familiar face, so he pets the dog.

> OLIVER (CON'T)
> Destiny, is that you, darling?

> VIOLET
> Oh, it's good that you two know each
> other. We are sorry to bother you, but
> we're locked out because of our little
> adventurer Destiny! So, the only thing
> that came to my mind was to knock on
> the next door.

> OLIVER
> Sure, sure... Are you with Mrs. Bendall?

> VIOLET
> Randall. Yes, I am her niece. Violet. My
> aunt is out of town for the weekend, and
> I'm here to take care of her dog, even if
> it doesn't seem so, right now. Well, once,
> I saw a small locksmith store down the
> street, on the way to the public park.
> Do you know him by any chance?

> OLIVER
> Locksmith? I'm afraid I don't.

Violet seems so hopeless.

> OLIVER (CON'T)
> Oh, God, I'm so sorry. You wanna come in?
> Don't stand there with that... With that...
> > (won't say "nightgown")
> I mean, with the dog.

Violet has no other choice.

> VIOLET
> Thank you--

> OLIVER
> You can call me "Oliver." That's what
> my friends call me. Cause, in fact, that
> is my name!

Oliver CHUCKLES. Violet barely smiles. Oliver grabs his coat and heads for the stairs.

> OLIVER (CON'T)
> So, I'd better go down the street to
> chase up that locksmith guy.

> VIOLET
> Will you really do that for us? Shoot,
> we caused you so much trouble, Oliver.

> OLIVER
> Come on, when did the morning jog
> become a bad thing? There's fresh
> coffee in the kitchen, and a sweatshirt,
> in case you feel cold. And please ignore
> all the dirt and mess in there, will you?

> VIOLET
> No worries. Everything can be cleaned
> right up. What matters most is to keep
> the heart clean.

They exchange a friendly smile. Oliver rushes down the stairs. The dog starts whining.

> VIOLET
> Stop whining. You are not going to the
> park till the evening.

EXT. OLIVER'S BUILDING – DAY

Oliver emerges from the building and rushes away. After a few seconds, a taxi arrives, and Jessica steps out. She enters the patisserie next to Oliver's building.

INT. LOCKSMITH STORE – DAY

The locksmith, RAUL, 60, walking with a limp, is looking through the jumbled drawers for something. Oliver strolls around while waiting for him.

                         OLIVER
              That Violet-girl is really lucky. I mean,
              I wasn't expecting to find the shop open
              on a Sunday. Her father's name must be
              "Luke," huh?

Oliver CHUCKLES. Raul gives him a blank stare.

                         OLIVER (CON'T)
              "Lucky Luke." The cartoon cowboy?

Raul finally finds his cellphone on a cluttered shelf.

                         RAUL
              That girl is lucky only because I am
              forgetful-Raul! I came all the way down
              here just to take this damn slavery device!

EXT. ENTRANCE, OLIVER'S BUILDING – DAY

Jessica, holding a fancy breakfast basket, searches her purse for Oliver's keys, but all she finds is her own key attached to a big letter "J." As she is about to buzz the intercom, the Redhead Woman opens the door to exit. She smiles and holds the door open for Jessica.

INT. FLOOR#2, OLIVER'S BUILDING – DAY

Jessica RINGS Oliver's doorbell. Violet, wearing Oliver's sweatshirt over her mini nightgown, opens the door with the dog in her arms.

                         JESSICA
              Surprise--

VIOLET
(simultaneously)
How fast--

Both are baffled. Jessica examines Violet from head to toe.

JESSICA
Indeed, he is fast!

VIOLET
(innocently)
What?

JESSICA
I can't believe this shit!

Violet takes a step back as Jessica throws the basket against the door. A green apple tumbles down the stairs.

VIOLET
If you're looking for Oliver--

JESSICA
Yeah, tell him to go to hell!

Jessica hurls her engagement ring to the ground and rushes down the stairs, fighting back tears.

VIOLET
But, wait, please! I think there is a huge misunderstanding here!

Angry HIGH HEELS can be HEARD. The building door SLAMS shut.

VIOLET
Oh, shoot...
(as the dog starts whining)
Stop whining. You are not going to the park till tomorrow.

FLASHBACK: EXT. STREETS, LONDON – DAY

The tower clock runs backwards at high speed…
Birds fly backwards around Westminster Abbey…
People jog backwards…
Traffic flows backwards on wet streets…
The morning sun appears behind a scudding cloud and illuminates the
shady city…
And we take a glance at the PARALLEL UNIVERSE…

FLASHBACK: INT. KITCHEN, VIOLET'S APARTMENT – DAY

Violet leans forward to grab her sociology book, carefully HOLDING
HER HAIR BACK to avoid getting it dipped into the milk. She tastes her
cereal, then turns off the sandwich maker. She studies the book while
eating her avocado toast. Lovely BUTTERFLY DRAWINGS can be seen
on the corner of the pages.

The dog licks the last crumbs in its bowl, then starts circling Violet.

> VIOLET
> No worries, sweetie. You'll be enjoying
> the park soon. But, first, let me make
> my stomach happy, too, huh?

FLASHBACK: INT. LIVING ROOM, OLIVER'S APARTMENT – DAY

The DOORBELL RINGS. Oliver quickly throws the dirty socks and shirts
behind the sofa.

> OLIVER
> I knew you were on the way to me, babe!

FLASHBACK: INT. FOYER, OLIVER'S APARTMENT – DAY

Oliver opens the door. Jessica is at the door with a fancy breakfast
basket.

JESSICA
Surprise!

OLIVER
And now the sun is officially up for
Oliver!

Oliver sets the basket down and passionately kisses Jessica. The basket leans to one side because of their bouncy feet. A green apple rolls down the foyer.

EXT. LOCKSMITH STREET – DAY

A tall young man in a good mood, CHARLES, 30, walks down the sidewalk while talking on his cellphone.

CHARLES
Be patient, man, you'll get it soon.
Don't worry. She definitely--

Oliver emerges from the locksmith store and bumps into Charles, causing him to drop the ring pouch in his hand.

OLIVER
Oh, so sorry, my friend!

Charles picks up the pouch and gestures at him, meaning "no problem," then keeps walking, talking on his phone.

CHARLES (CON'T)
She definitely will love it.

Raul closes the store, holding his toolbox. He and Oliver go down the sidewalk together. As they pass a FRECKLED BOY in a brown hooded top, 16, Oliver notices one of his sneakers is unlaced, so he warns him.

OLIVER
Careful, my friend!

The Freckled Boy quickly ties it up and rushes away.

EXT. HYDE PARK – DAY

Jessica sobs under a plane tree. Her cellphone VIBRATES. She doesn't answer it as the caller is "Honey."

                    JESSICA
          Scumbag!

People jogging in the park oddly glance at her. Jessica feels uncomfortable and leaves the park.

INT. FLOOR#2, OLIVER'S BUILDING – DAY

Raul is changing the deadbolt on Violet's door.

Violet, with a ponytail and dressed, waits in the hallway with the dog in her arms. Oliver's apartment door is also open.

Oliver toys with Jessica's engagement ring while waiting for Jessica to answer his call. There is no response. Oliver smacks his fist against the wall. It hurts.

                    VIOLET
          She doesn't answer, right? Shoot, that's
          all because of me!

                    OLIVER
          Well, I thought it was the dog.

The dog's ears are pricked.

                    VIOLET
          I know I blamed Destiny before, just
          like every weakling and coward would
          do! Shifting the blame to destiny is the
          easiest way to escape from our own
          foolish mistakes!

                    OLIVER
          Are we still talking about the dog here?

                    VIOLET
          I mean, the truth is, I was the one who
          messed everything up today. I am the
          guilty one.

                    OLIVER
          Yeah? How so?

                    VIOLET
          I acted without awareness the whole
          morning. First, I dipped my hair in
          the cereal bowl and left the kitchen
          to clean it up. Then, the bread in that
          shabby toaster burned and I panicked
          because of the smoke alarm. So, I opened
          the kitchen window and then rushed
          to open the apartment door to get rid
          of the smoke, completely forgetting
          about the dog. And the door slammed
          shut in my face because of the strong
          airflow I created with my own hands.

                    OLIVER
          Yeah, it's really like a crime wave.
          So, what did the police say?

The two share a bittersweet smile.

                    VIOLET
          Just let me know if there is anything
          I can do to help you and your fiancée
          work things out.

                    OLIVER
          Thanks, Violet, but it's not gonna be
          necessary. Jessica responds to my calls
          no matter what. I know her. I bet her
          phone was in silent mode or something.

Oliver makes another call to Jessica. His call is REJECTED this time.

Oliver kicks the wall. It hurts. Raul grabs his toolbox and SHUTS Violet's door, causing the two to startle.

                         RAUL
          My job is done here!

                         VIOLET
          Oh, thank you, sir. You've saved my life.

                         RAUL
          Here are your new keys. You'd better
          put one of them around your neck. It
          might help you survive without assistance.
                    (to Oliver)
          And you'd better find your fiancée and
          talk to her properly instead of constantly
          bruising yourself around.

Violet and Oliver exchange a look while Raul limps down the stairs.

FLASHBACK: EXT. LOCKSMITH STREET – DAY

Violet, her hair loose, walks the dog towards the public park.

Charles walks down the sidewalk, talking on his cellphone and toying with a ring pouch in his hand.

                         CHARLES
          Be patient, man, you'll get it soon.
          Don't worry. She definitely will love it.

While passing Violet, Charles notices her beauty. Raul puts his cellphone into his pocket and locks the locksmith store. All of a sudden, the Freckled Boy with a brown hooded top pushes Violet down and runs off with her purse.

                         VIOLET
          Oh, no! Help! He took my purse!
          He took my purse!

Charles turns around and sees Violet crawling on the ground and trying to hold the dog's leash.

                    VIOLET (CON'T)
              Please, catch him! Please!

Charles runs after the Freckled Boy. Raul helps Violet.

The Freckled Boy searches through the purse while running away. As he stumbles because of his unlaced sneaker, Charles grabs him by the neck. The Freckled Boy tosses the purse at his face and dashes into an alley.

People around Charles APPLAUD and WHISTLE, which surprises him. A BEARDED OLD MAN, 70, proudly taps him on the shoulder.

                    BEARDED OLD MAN
              Well done, young man! The world is in
              need of more people like you!

FLASHBACK: EXT. HYDE PARK – DAY

Beneath a plane tree, Jessica feeds Oliver pastries while enjoying her green apple. People jogging in the park can't help but smile as they pass by their cute picnic.

FLASHBACK: INT. LOCKSMITH STORE – DAY

Raul applies first aid to Violet's injured elbow.
Charles sees them through the window and enters with Violet's purse.

                    VIOLET
              Oh, God, I can't believe you brought it
              back! Thank you!

Violet simply looks into her purse and heaves a sigh of relief.

                    CHARLES
No problem at all. If you need medical
attention, there is a community clinic
about two hundred meters away.

                    VIOLET
No, it doesn't hurt that much. Oh, we
haven't officially met yet, right? My
name is Violet, and this very kind man
is Raul. It's a pleasure to meet you both.

                    CHARLES
Charles. May I suggest you check that
bag more properly, Violet?

                    VIOLET
Why? You mean... That boy might've
picked something from my purse?

                    RAUL
Save your breath and dig in!

Violet checks her purse more properly.

                    VIOLET
Oh, I think you are right, Charles.
My wallet is not here.

                    RAUL
Have fun at the cop-shop!

The dog's ears are pricked.

                    VIOLET
I now have to file a report, right?
Shoot! Is there any police station
in this neighborhood?

                    CHARLES
The nearest one is about six hundred
meters away.

As a final touch, Raul applies a band-aid on Violet's arm while mumbling about Charles.

> RAUL
> Such an organic GPS!

Violet smiles. Charles simply shrugs his shoulders.

INT. LIVING ROOM, JESSICA'S APARTMENT – DAY

Jessica eats a bucket of ice cream with a soup spoon while pacing back and forth. As she hears TIRE SQUEAL, she peers through the curtains. She sees Oliver getting out of his car and walking towards her building. Jessica angrily sits on the sofa and ignores the insistently BUZZING DOORBELL.

EXT. ENTRANCE, JESSICA'S BUILDING – DAY

Oliver looks up at the third floor, buzzing the intercom.

> OLIVER
> Jessica! Come on, babe, we need to
> talk! It's not what you think! It's just
> your mischievous imagination! Come
> on, let me in!

INT. LIVING ROOM, JESSICA'S APARTMENT – DAY

Jessica's cellphone VIBRATES. The caller is "Honey." As Jessica angrily throws the cellphone against a wall, it's broken in half.

EXT. ENTRANCE, JESSICA'S BUILDING – DAY

Oliver KNOCKS on the entrance door, yet there is no one to open it for him. He kicks the door. He notices some residents looking at him with pity behind their windows.

INT. LIVING ROOM, JESSICA'S APARTMENT – DAY

The sound of a CAR ENGINE is HEARD. Jessica sees Oliver's car speeding away. She sits on the sofa, then suddenly throws the ice cream bucket toward the curtains.

>   JESSICA
>   Go to the hellhole where you belong!

Jessica curls up on the sofa, shedding silent tears.

FLASHBACK: INT. POLICE STATION – DAY

Crowded... Noisy dialogues, printers, ringing phones... Police officers are working at their desks. Violet fills out an official form on a bench. The dog is curled up at her feet. Charles arrives with two paper cups of coffee.

>   CHARLES
>   Some coffee?

>   VIOLET
>   Oh, very kind of you.

Violet takes a sip. Charles sits next to her and offers her some creamer and sugar packs.

>   CHARLES
>   Not sure how you like it.

>   VIOLET
>   It's perfect the way it is. Thank you,
>   Charles. Forgive me for keeping you
>   busy on Sunday.

>   CHARLES
>   No problem at all.

>   VIOLET
>   So, who are you? What you do?

CHARLES
Me? I am a construction worker.

VIOLET
Really? Dangerous job.

CHARLES
Not so much, as long as you keep yourself
on the safe side.

Violet agrees with a nod and then glances at her watch.

VIOLET
When do you think they will take our
testimony?

Charles scans the surrounding crowd.

CHARLES
It seems like we'll have enough time
for our second coffee.

VIOLET
Oh, shoot... Okay, so let's shorten the
process.

Violet takes a big sip of her coffee. Charles likes her joke and takes a big
sip of his own.

Two OFFICERS in their late thirties, one BLONDE and one BRUNETTE,
wearily escort a CRIMINAL to the detention room. Violet sighs sadly.

VIOLET
I really don't get what the purpose
of stealing is.

CHARLES
Maintaining life, of course. What else?

VIOLET
And do they call it "living"?

CHARLES
What is that supposed to mean?

VIOLET
It's very hard to talk about a meaningful
life if there is a soul constantly being
damaged.

CHARLES
What damage?

VIOLET
These people assume they are only
causing harm to others. They are
completely unaware of their self-harm.

CHARLES
Well, we can't judge people without
knowing their stories.

VIOLET
Yes, but witnessing this mess around us
makes me sick at heart. And this is only
a tiny part of the wreckage. If Lydians
could have watched today's newscasts
beforehand, they would never have
invented money.

CHARLES
Are you telling me it's possible to survive
without money? Cause I can assure you
that there's no such world, Violet.

VIOLET
I was talking about the nasty ways
to obtain it.

CHARLES
Eh, what you gonna do? No other chance
for the little crumbs trapped in the
merciless wheels of capitalism.

                    VIOLET
Only if they believe they are nothing
but crumbs.

                    CHARLES
Oh, really? So, tell me what you are,
Violet? You may be a princess with
a perfect life, but let me remind you
that not everyone is as lucky as you!

                    VIOLET
It's nothing to do with luck, Charles.
It's about your perspective on life.

                    CHARLES
Perspective? Just that simple, huh? And
what about fate? It's not a tiny bug you
can easily escape. You know that, right?

                    VIOLET
Fate is surely not a bug. It is more likely a
handy excuse to curse during tough times.

                    CHARLES
How is that again?

                    VIOLET
We tend to blame fate when we feel stuck
in life. But it's quickly forgotten while we
are busy being proud of ourselves, even
for a tiny little success. Haven't you ever
noticed?

Charles finishes his coffee and simply crumples the cup.

                    VIOLET (CON'T)
We love playing the victim, even though
we are strong and smart beings capable
of writing our own destinies.

                    CHARLES
          It's unbelievable how easily you
          oversimplify destiny, as if it were
          some kind of notebook.

                    VIOLET
          Actually, it is. An invisible one.

Charles mockingly shakes his head.

                    CHARLES
          So tell me please, do we also have a
          "magical pen" to write down on that
          "invisible notebook"?

                    VIOLET
                (displaying her pen)
          We sure have. And it consists of three
          major elements.

Charles watches her in astonishment while Violet unscrews the pen.
She displays the pen nib.

                    VIOLET (CON'T)
          Awareness...

She removes the pen's bottom along with the ink chamber.

                    VIOLET (CON'T)
          Moral conscience...

She finally displays the body of the pen.

                    VIOLET (CON'T)
          And, free will.

                    CHARLES
          So, these three elements will let me
          determine all the events I'll encounter
          in life, huh?

                    VIOLET
No. They will let you determine your
reactions to them.

Violet begins to reassemble the pen.

                    CHARLES
You are an interesting girl, I have to say.

                    VIOLET
I am just a girl who tends to question life.

                    CHARLES
...and who hates money.

                    VIOLET
Let's say I'm not crazy about it. I mean,
it can't be a goal, but just a tool.

                    CHARLES
A tool that we all need, Violet. Come on,
you also must be praying for some cash
once in a while, right? Like winning the
lottery or something.

                    VIOLET
Not really. There is nothing we can truly
own in this world, so what's the point?

                    CHARLES
Come on, Violet, you went too far now.
What about our cars, or our furniture,
huh? Whose are they? Or this dull coat on
me, and even these arms or this crooked
nose? Who can say these aren't mine?

                    VIOLET
So you are one of those people who borrow
a book without even thinking of returning it.

Charles' mind wanders. He pretends to take a puff on his unlit cigarette, believing that it helps him calm down.

                    CHARLES
          So, we have nothing, huh? Zero, zilch,
          nothing!

                    VIOLET
          In my opinion, we have one real treasure
          to invest in. Our souls. Because only our
          souls belong to us forever and ever.

                    CHARLES
          Okay, I'm now convinced that you've been
          living under a rock!

                    VIOLET
          And what's that supposed to mean?

                    CHARLES
          It means the world is messed up, Violet!
          There is a very complicated puzzle out
          there right now, and you are talking about
          eternity here! While you are protesting
          against small robberies and mumbling
          about those Lydian guys, the world keeps
          sinking into a huge whirlpool! Innocent
          children are losing their lives because of
          those various types of wars in every corner
          of the world!

                    VIOLET
          ...which aim at filling some pockets that
          are already full, right?

Instead of responding her, Charles tosses his crumpled coffee cup into a waste bin.

VIOLET (CON'T)
Our history teacher used to say that
"the oldest enemy of humankind is the
excessive greed of humankind itself."
I mean, can't you just see it, Charles?
If we can't solve the puzzle within us
first, we'll never be able to solve the
one out there.

Charles pretends to take another puff on his unlit cigarette. The Blonde Officer gestures at him, "not permitted." An upset Charles shows him that it's unlit and then places the cigarette behind his ear.

CHARLES
Okay, Violet, well said. Let me ask you
a simple question then. Since you care
about the "soul investment" that much,
and you are not a fan of materialism,
"obviously," then why are you spending
your precious time here for your stolen
wallet, huh?

VIOLET
For security reasons, of course. My ID
card was in the wallet.

CHARLES
So then you asked for help like crazy,
only because of your ID?

VIOLET
No... Because there was something very
valuable in my purse...

CHARLES
A-ha, you see? I knew it!

VIOLET (CON'T)
Something irreplaceable.

Violet pulls an old photograph out of her purse.

In the PHOTO: A YOUNG VIOLET, 17, stands in front of an old village house with her BROTHER, 10, SISTER, 8, her frail MOTHER, 35, and grumpy FATHER, 40.

Charles sits, looking at the photo with interest.

                    VIOLET (CON'T)
          The only picture of my family. All the
          others burned down in a big fire. Along
          with our house... And my whole family...

                    CHARLES
          No, shit...

                    VIOLET
          I was seventeen by then. I was in the city
          that weekend, visiting my aunt. Now, you
          can decide whether I'm lucky or not.
          I suppose it depends on your perspective...

                    CHARLES
                  (simultaneously)
          Perspective...

A FEMALE OFFICER, 50, invites Violet to her desk.

                    FEMALE OFFICER
          Hey, Miss! Proceed!

The dog's ears are pricked. Violet gets to her feet, finishes her coffee, and gently throws the cup into the waste bin. She turns to Charles and smiles.

                    VIOLET
          Let's?

INT. LIVING ROOM, PATRICK'S HOUSE – NIGHT

A retro-style living room with an open kitchen. There are many vintage records, but no record player.

Happy family photos of Oliver, Jessica, Patrick, and Patrick's late wife are fixed on the fridge door with car-shaped magnets.

Oliver's father, PATRICK, 60, sets up a beautiful dinner table for three, mumbling the song "Too Much." The OVEN TIMER is HEARD. Patrick takes the tray out and smells the fish.

A KNOCK at the door. Patrick happily opens it.

> PATRICK
> Right on time! Delicious fish are ready,
> just for three!

An upset Oliver enters, clutching a wine bottle.

> OLIVER
> Good news, dad! We can have one fish
> and a half each!

Patrick scans the front porch. Jessica is not around. Oliver pops the cork and pours himself some wine.

INT. LIVING ROOM, JESSICA'S APARTMENT – NIGHT

Jessica, curled up on the sofa, awakens to a TIRE SQUEAL. She peeps through the curtains. This time, it's not Oliver's car. She picks up the ice cream bucket lying on the floor, then sits at her laptop. While working, she nervously eats biscuits and drinks the melted ice cream.

INT. LIVING ROOM, PATRICK'S HOUSE – NIGHT

Patrick and Oliver are at the silent dinner table. Their meals are rarely touched. Oliver involuntarily keeps tapping his fist on the table, lost in his thoughts.

> PATRICK
> Have you lost your tongue or what?
> Come on, son, spill the beans.

OLIVER
You know what I figured out today, dad?
Jessica never really got to know me. And
that's the core of my problem here.

PATRICK
Son, I'm already tired of doing crossword
puzzles all week. Just tell me the reason
for the fight. Maybe there is something
I can do to help, huh?

Oliver shakes his head no. He then finishes his wine and pours a refill.

PATRICK (CON'T)
Is it because of your financial issues? Is it
the mortgage? Or furnishing? What is it?

OLIVER
I don't want to talk about it, dad. Please.

PATRICK
(sharp-tongue)
Or maybe she was pissed off for a good
reason, huh? We both know how cranky
you can get when you are under stress.

OLIVER
Dad, I told you I did nothing wrong! It's
her choice to ignore me! So, please, just...
Just don't worry about me, okay?

PATRICK
Ask me that again once you see your
ghastly face in the mirror!

Both sighs in desperation. Patrick looks at his late wife's photo on the wall and sighs.

PATRICK (CON'T)
Despite all those hefty challenges we
faced, your mother and I shared a very
happy life together for twenty-eight
years, seven months, and twelve days...

OLIVER
(simultaneously)
And twelve days...

Patrick wipes his small tears with the back of his hand.

PATRICK
We could always found a way to make
each other laugh, no matter what kind
of trouble we had been through.

OLIVER
Dad, I am your son. I am not you. And
Jessica is nothing like my mom. So,
nothing is the same here.

PATRICK
The passion between you two is the same,
son. I saw that flame the very first time
I saw you two lovebirds together.

OLIVER
Then our flame has gone far beyond its
purpose, dad. It burned everything down.

PATRICK
Then start mixing some cement to rebuild
it. You two belong to each other and will
be bonded at heart since you both have
those rings on your fingers.

He points at Oliver's engagement ring. Oliver slowly opens his fist, and
Jessica's engagement ring appears in his palm.

                    OLIVER
          Hell yeah...

INT. A SHADY ROOM – NIGHT

A man's hand in a black glove is toying with a silver-gray jackknife. On the side is a black, full-face ski mask.

INT. LIVING ROOM, OLIVER'S APARTMENT – NIGHT

The room is illuminated only by the laptop's screen. Among the empty coffee cups, Oliver is sending a flood of emails to Jessica.

INT. BEDROOM, PATRICK'S HOUSE – NIGHT

Patrick, in his pajamas, carefully examines the amounts in his passbook and smiles. He then places a red ribbon and the passbook in the pocket of an old-fashioned gray suit. He hangs the suit and goes to bed. When he switches off the bedside lamp, the room is enveloped in darkness.

FLASHBACK: INT. LIVING ROOM, PATRICK'S HOUSE – NIGHT

Oliver, Jessica, and Patrick are at the end of their fish- menu dinner. A lilac envelope rests on the table. Oliver and Jessica cheerfully dance around the room while Patrick wipes his happy tears with a lilac handkerchief.

EXT. PATRICK'S NEIGHBORHOOD – DAY

Patrick, in his old-fashioned gray suit, emerges from his one-story house and locks its door. He fondly caresses the snowdrop flower in a large pot on the front porch.

                    PATRICK
          How are you today, dolly?

His next-door neighbor, MRS. HOWARD, 55, a belly Afro- British woman in a sweatsuit, waves goodbye to her husband, who drives away to work. She notices Patrick.

> MRS. HOWARD
> Oh, Mister Marlow, hello!

> PATRICK
> Good morning, Mrs. Howard.

> MRS. HOWARD
> What on earth is this? Or have you decided
> to return to work?

They spontaneously walk down the sidewalk together. Mrs. Howard speaks enthusiastically, not allowing Patrick to speak at all.

> MRS. HOWARD
> Haven't I told you that you're still young
> for retirement?
> (GIGGLES)
> Oh, time is the biggest liar, Mister Marlow,
> believe me. As you can see, I go for a stroll
> every morning, regardless of what it
> mumbles in my ear!
> (GIGGLES)
> So, why are you all suited up so early, huh?
> Oh, speaking of style, how is my lovely
> Jessica? And my dear Oliver must be busy
> as usual. I haven't seen him since he moved
> out. Oh, we still haven't received any wedding
> invitation. Haven't they set the date yet?

> PATRICK
> Not yet, but soon--

> MRS. HOWARD
> Oh, good! Cause the outfit I ordered is
> suitable for winter!

They reach the park.

MRS. HOWARD (CON'T)
Well, this is me! It was great chatting with
you, Mister Marlow!

She heads for the walking path while Patrick continues on his way.

PATRICK
Likewise...

INT. OLIVER'S CAR – DAY

Oliver, in a black suit, stops the car to let the schoolkids cross the street. Kids wave at him thankfully. The cute smile on Oliver's face disappears when he notices the fuel gauge is FLASHING RED.

EXT. SIDEWALK CAFÉ – DAY

MIGUEL, 45, a thin Colombian man, sweeps away the dry leaves in the entryway. He sees Patrick in a rush.

MIGUEL
Hey, Señor! Where were you all weekend?
Come on in, have a cup of coffee! It's
freezing today!

PATRICK
Thanks, Miguel! I need to get to the bank
right away!

MIGUEL
To the bank? But they are not even open yet!

Patrick checks his watch. Miguel is correct.

EXT. GAS STATION – DAY

Oliver's car is being refueled. Oliver checks the fuel gauge to make sure the tank is full.

INT. JESSICA'S OFFICE, TEXTILE COMPANY – DAY

It's a clean and organized office. The nameplate reads "JESSICA BAYLEY-FOREIGN TRADE SPECIALIST."

Jessica, in a black dress, enters and sits at her laptop while nervously eating a large sandwich. NANCY, 25, the company secretary, KNOCKS on the open door and enters.

                    NANCY
          Good morning, Miss Bayley. Oh, you
          look kind of pale today. Is everything
          alright?

                    JESSICA
          Everything will be perfect if you tell
          me the schedule, Nancy!

                    NANCY
          Yes, sure... The lunch reservation was
          confirmed. The restaurant manager was
          reminded of the special sauce and risotto,
          as you pleased. Conference hall is all set
          up, and the cocktail lounge will be ready
          in about twenty minutes.

                    JESSICA
          So far, so good. Let's work now.

                    NANCY
          And, your fiancée, I mean Mister Marlow
          called three times. He is waiting for your
          call.

                    JESSICA
               (mumbles to herself)
          Yeah, in his dreams!
               (to Nancy)
          If he calls again, tell him I'm in a
          crucial meeting. Bye, Nancy!

Nancy turns to exit, but then stops and turns around.

> NANCY
> Excuse me, Miss Bayley, it's not my
> business, but he sounded quite upset.
> I mean, there may be a serious issue
> or something.

> JESSICA
> You are right, Nancy. It's definitely none
> of your business!

> NANCY
> Yes, of course... I'm sorry.

> JESSICA
> If you don't want to be more sorry, do
> not transfer any calls from Oliver! Got
> it? "Never!" You want me to write it
> down for you?

Nancy simply shakes her head no. She goes to her desk in the lobby area. A nervous Jessica takes a big bite of her sandwich while dealing with a thick folder.

An enthusiastic young man, ARTHUR, 35, enters while eating peanuts.

> ARTHUR
> Jessica! Wow, you've finally discovered
> the joy of breakfast, huh? Welcome to
> the club!

> JESSICA
> Morning, Arthur.

While talking, Arthur randomly touches the fabric samples and bulletin boards on the walls.

ARTHUR
It's a fabulous morning, indeed! The
driver has just told me that the Italians
seemed extremely happy yesterday
morning, despite the fact that their flight
was delayed an hour. I'm guessing the
reason was that you booked the same
hotel they had enjoyed on their previous
stay, huh?

JESSICA
Maybe...

ARTHUR
I am curious how you managed to find
four available rooms in that fabulous hotel
during this busy fair season, Jessica. You
must own one of those... umm, what do
they call it? A-ha! A "magic wand," right?

JESSICA
Maybe... Although some people call it
"early booking".

Arthur CHUCKLES. Jessica adjusts the bulletin board on the wall, which
became asymmetrical because of his touches, and then she returns to
her laptop. Arthur wanders around, trying not to touch anything.

ARTHUR
I'm really looking forward to today's
meeting! Think about it, Jessica! If
we can convince them about our new
project, we will take our collaboration
to a fabulous level! We may even become
the most famous textile company on
the continent in the blink of an eye!

JESSICA
Maybe...

ARTHUR
After inspecting the conference hall, I'll
accompany the driver to the hotel to
pick up our guests. It means that you
don't have much time to arrange a
fabulous welcome party for them, huh?

JESSICA
Don't worry. I practiced with a great
farewell party yesterday.

ARTHUR
What?

JESSICA
Everything was already arranged in
a perfect way, Arthur. Including their
favorite cocktails.

ARTHUR
Well, I forgot for a moment that Jessica
Bayley is behind the wheel. Everything
is gonna be fabulous today, Jessica!
I can feel it in my bones!
(checks the time)
Oh, I better get going now!

Arthur rushes out of the office while Jessica deletes Oliver's emails without even reading them.

JESSICA
Fabulous...

INT. SIDEWALK CAFÉ – DAY

A simple coffee shop. Not crowded. A short foot-boy, BEAVER, 18, wipes the counter. Miguel and Patrick enter.

                    MIGUEL
          Hey, Beaver, bring us coffee! Make
          sure it's hot and strong!

Beaver bows. BULLDOZER, 25, a bulky guy of Romanian origin, is filling
out a lotto coupon at a table.

                    PATRICK
          Look who's here! Bulldozer! How is
          my boy doing nowadays?

                    BULLDOZER
Same as always, sir. Horsing around the daytime, flowing to the streets
at the nighttime.

                    PATRICK
          Nobody said life was an easy game.

                    BULLDOZER
          Ever...

Patrick fatherly taps Bulldozer on the shoulder. Miguel and Patrick sit
at another table. Beaver serves them coffee and biscuits with a big
smile that reveals his buckteeth.

FLASHBACK: JESSICA'S OFFICE, TEXTILE COMPANY – DAY

Jessica, in a lilac dress, sips her coffee while dealing with a thick folder.
Arthur randomly touches the fabric samples and bulletin boards on the
walls while talking.

                    ARTHUR
          Everything is gonna be fabulous today,
          Jessica! I can feel it in my bones!

                    JESSICA
          Be careful, Arthur. Some people call
          it "rheumatism!"

They GIGGLE. Arthur checks his watch.

ARTHUR
Oh, I better get going now!

JESSICA
See you!

Arthur rushes away. Jessica adjusts the bulletin board on the wall.

FLASHBACK: INT. CAR SHOWROOM – DAY

Crowded due to the campaign prices. Oliver, in a gray suit, explains the features of a car to a customer, MISS CARTER, 40. She is a curvy woman with a lovely face. She toys with her cleavage necklace, while listening.

OLIVER
...And its speed control system is one
of the best, Miss Carter.

MISS CARTER
Oh, that's fantastic! And, what does that
thing do?

OLIVER
Let's say you are driving a long distance.
Your car maintains a constant speed. If
it approaches another vehicle from behind--

MISS CARTER
(GIGGLES)
Oh, for shame!

OLIVER
Well, in that case, the system automatically
reduces the speed. And once the vehicle
in front of you moves out of your way,
you regain your previous speed.

MISS CARTER
Oh, that's fantastic! I surely need that speed
control thing. I go off the rails every so often.

She GIGGLES. Oliver forces a smile.

                    OLIVER
          So, would you prefer a sedan, or a
          hatchback?

                    MISS CARTER
          Definitely a hatchback. Curvy figures
          are more desirable, don't you think?

                    OLIVER
          There's no accounting for taste, Miss
          Carter. However, my good colleague
          Bryan may bring a new approach here.
          Let's see.

A successful salesperson, BRYAN, 30, is saying goodbye to a customer at the entrance door. As Oliver gestures at him, Bryan goes there instantly.

                    BRYAN
          Yes, boss?

                    OLIVER
          Bryan, could you please explain our special
          offers in detail to Miss Carter?

A disappointed Miss Carter stops toying with her necklace.

                    BRYAN
          That would be my pleasure. My desk is right
          over there, Miss Carter. Please, after you...

                    MISS CARTER
          Oh, okay then... Thank you, Oliver.

                    OLIVER
          Thanks to you, Miss Carter. Enjoy your
          curvy car.

Oliver makes a call while walking towards his office.

OLIVER
Hey, babe, how is it going? No, I just
wanted to give my support to my sweet
babe on her biggy presentation. By the
way, she'd better be sure those macaroni
guys keep their eyes on the screen at all
times.

Oliver enters his office. There is a long, thin CRACK on its glass door. A nameplate reads "OLIVER MARLOW — SALES MANAGER."

FLASHBACK: Int. JESSICA'S OFFICE, TEXTILE COMPANY – Day

Jessica, in a lilac dress, works on her presentation diagrams while talking on her cellphone.

JESSICA
Please, hon, don't start. I'm already
nervous here. Yes, hon,I'll call you
once it's over. Well, I'll definitely make
history today. Why? Because I heard
your magical voice… No, I'm not teasing…
No, I'm not…
(GIGGLES)
Okay, hon, enough with the flirt-break.
I really have to go now. Thanks, hon.
Love you big.

Nancy KNOCKS on the door, holding a mug.

JESSICA
Hey, Nancy, what you have there?

NANCY
I prepared my grandma's mint tea recipe
for you, Miss Bayley. I mean, for your
vocal cords.

Both GIGGLE.

> JESSICA
> You shouldn't bother. Thanks.

Jessica sips her mint tea. It tastes good.

> JESSICA (CON'T)
> You know what, Nancy? If you don't
> want to get more tired around here,
> you shouldn't create new habits for us.

INT. OLIVER'S OFFICE – DAY

Oliver, in a black suit, sits at his computer, unable to concentrate. When he minimizes the page, Jessica's smiling photo appears on the screensaver. Oliver makes a call.

> OLIVER
> Hi, Nancy! Yes, it's me again! Jessica
> isn't there yet?

INTERCUT WITH NANCY AT HER DESK:

While on the phone, Nancy glances at Jessica's office. Jessica, in a black dress, is dealing with a tick folder.

> NANCY
> No. I mean, yes, she is, but I'm afraid
> I can't put you through.

Nancy timidly gestures at Jessica, meaning that "Oliver is on the line." Jessica angrily scribbles a big "NO!" on a paper and holds it up. Nancy has to lie to Oliver.

> NANCY (CON'T)
> Well... Because she is in a crucial meeting
> right now.

INTERCUT WITH OLIVER IN HIS OFFICE:

Oliver paces back and forth, talking on his cellphone.

                    OLIVER
          What meeting? I thought those Italians
          wouldn't be there before noon! Oh, this
          one was arranged at the last moment,
          huh? Okay, okay, I got it!

The GENERAL MANAGER of the showroom, 55, passes by Oliver's office. Bryan catches him, and the two amble along, conversing. Oliver doesn't notice them.

                    OLIVER (CON'T)
          Tell Jessica to call me back as soon as
          the meeting ends! If she is really in one!

Oliver hangs up the phone and severely kicks the door, causing the thin crack to spread all over the glass. The General Manager appears behind the cracked glass. Bryan appears right behind him. Oliver grins guiltily.

                    OLIVER
          Nothing to worry about, sir. Everything
          is under control.

The cracked glass LOUDLY BREAKS into smithereens. Oliver clumsily pushes the glass shards aside with his foot.

                    OLIVER (CON'T)
          Or "under construction," we can say.

INT. SIDEWALK CAFÉ – DAY

Miguel and Patrick sip coffee and talk. Bulldozer overhears their conversation while reading a sports paper.

                    MIGUEL
          Sorry to hear this, Señor. I hope they'll
          make it up soon.

                    PATRICK
          They will, Miguel, they will. I'm sure my
          cranky son irritated Jessica in some way.

                    MIGUEL
But Oliver is so in love with Jessica.
Why would he upset her?

                    PATRICK
Because of the most dangerous thing
for human body.

                    MIGUEL
Carbs?

                    PATRICK
Stress. I bet that he is in financial crisis,
but afraid to tell me. So, as a father,
I need to solve this issue right away.

                    MIGUEL
How?

                    PATRICK
My retirement bonus is sleeping in the
bank just like that. I'll withdraw it and
give it to them.

                    MIGUEL
But you worked your whole life to deserve
that bonus, Señor.

                    PATRICK
Frankly, Miguel, I don't feel like I worked
at all. Being a teacher was always a
pleasure for me. I was planning to open
a savings account for my grandkids in
the future anyway.
          (secretly wipes his tiny tears)
It's not a huge sum, but I hope that it will
be enough to let my son breathe again
and focus back on his relationship.

                    MIGUEL
Still, it's your money, Señor.

                    PATRICK
          I own nothing but my responsibilities,
          Miguel. Capitalism has ruined way too
          many relationships by now. I won't let
          it hunt my son's as well.

Patrick finishes his coffee and checks the time.

                    PATRICK
          Oh, we said one cup, yet we've finished
          the whole pot, huh?

                    MIGUEL
          Are you going to the bank now?

                    PATRICK
          Right after checking out the plumbing,
          one last time.

Patrick goes to the restroom.

A tall young man, LIAM, 25, steps in. He sits at Bulldozer's table and hands him some lottery tickets.

Miguel glances at them for a long moment, then joins them at their table, offering them biscuits. Beaver serves them coffee, and the four engage in conversation.

INT. OLIVER'S OFFICE – DAY

A HOUSEKEEPER, 50, sweeps away the glass shards into a dustpan. Oliver holds a garbage bag to help her. Bryan rushes into the office while on the phone.

                    BRYAN
          Okay, just a sec, just a sec!
                    (to Oliver)
          Hey, boss! The glazier says that they
          are extremely busy today!

The General Manager glances at the damaged door while passing Oliver's office. Oliver bows, half-respectfully and half-ashamed. Once he is out of his sight, Oliver responds to Bryan:

> OLIVER
> Tell him I'll pay double if they fix it today!
> And I want frosted glass this time!

Bryan rushes away while on the phone.

> BRYAN
> You heard my boss, right?

The Housekeeper takes the garbage bag out. Oliver shuffles over to his messy desk.

INT. BANK – DAY

Patrick signs some official papers. A FEMALE BANK CLERK hands him a bank deposit bag. The label on it reads, "MR. PATRICK MARLOW." Patrick delicately ties the deposit bag with a red ribbon.

EXT. ALLEY#1 – DAY

A police car is parked near a burning house. In order to make room for the fire truck, a tow truck removes a yellowish jalopy parked at the no-parking zone.

EXT. BANK STREET – DAY

Patrick emerges from the bank with the deposit bag under his arm. He makes a call, heading for the bus shelter.

> PATRICK
> How are you, son? Well, I'm doing
> excellent. I'm planning to visit you at
> work today. I've got a surprise for you.

He CHUCKLES.

> PATRICK (CON'T)
> No, no, all fish are happy and free at
> the moment. I'll tell you what it is
> when I get there.

INTERCUT WITH OLIVER'S IN HIS OFFICE:

The tall glazier is measuring the door frame. Oliver is printing out some documents, talking on his cellphone.

> OLIVER
> Dad, please stop worrying about me.
> I am fine. And don't bother coming all
> the way down here. I have no time to
> breathe today. You stay at home. I'll
> try to stop by toward evening, okay?

INTERCUT WITH PATRICK AT THE BUS SHELTER:

A disappointed Patrick is talking on his cellphone.

> PATRICK
> Okay, son... If you say so.

Patrick leaves the bus shelter to walk back home. Rain clouds gather in the sky.

FLASHBACK: INT. YELLOWISH JALOPY – DAY

Charles pulls up near the COLLEGE BUILDING. He tidies his hair. Violet, in a pink skirt suit, emerges from the dorm and gets in the car with a genuine smile.

> CHARLES
> Wow, you look amazingly ready for
> the interview, huh?

VIOLET
Thank you, Charles. I hope I am.

CHARLES
By the way, what's your major in college?

VIOLET
Sociology.

Charles smiles admiringly, driving off.

MINUTES LATER:

LIGHTNINGS FLASH. Charles's car sputters out at the red lights at the CROSSROADS near the subway station.

CHARLES
No, come on, not now!

Charles desperately tries to restart the engine. Violet checks her watch, getting late for her interview.

VIOLET
I'd better take the subway.

CHARLES
No, no, I promised I'd drive you there,
and I will.

HORNS BLARE, as the lights turn green. Charles repeatedly declutches and turns the key. The engine finally starts, but then stops again.
A SHARP CLAP of THUNDER.

HALF AN HOUR LATER:

It's drizzling. Charles is waiting in his car near the ADVERTISING AGENCY BUILDING.

Violet emerges from the building, covering her hair bun with her purse. She is surprised to see the yellowish jalopy and rushes in it. Charles hands her a tissue box.

VIOLET
Thanks! So, you have finally won the
battle, huh? Congratulations!

CHARLES
Yeah. Two minutes after you ran into
the subway station. So, tell me how
your interview went. What did they say?

VIOLET
Oh, they said "punctuality is the soul of
business," and they politely showed me
the way out.

CHARLES
No, shit!
        (punches the wheel)
I should already send this bloody rust
bucket to the junkyard! Shit!

VIOLET
Don't upset yourself, Charles. After all,
everything happens for a reason.

CHARLES
What reason? Don't you see how I ruined
your life in less than an hour!

VIOLET
Ruined? Is it certainty or a prediction?

CHARLES
Okay, I certainly know is that I now owe
you a cool job. So, why don't we grab a
bite and talk some business, huh, if you
have time?

VIOLET
Sure. I am unemployed as a bird.

Violet smiles. Charles drives away with a bittersweet smile on his face.

EXT. PATRICK'S HOUSE – DAY

Patrick arrives home with the deposit bag under his arm. As he is about to unlock the door of his house, he senses something weird and turns around. Four ski-masked burglars in black are staring at him.

The FIRST BURGLAR, a tall figure, reaches out.

> BURGLAR#1
> Hand me the bag, old chap!

Patrick reflexively throws his cellphone at him. It hits the First Burglar's head and then falls into the large flowerpot. As Patrick tries to flee, three of them run him down and severely kick him.

> BURGLAR#1
> You asked for it!

The FORTH BURGLAR, a short figure, snoops around. The other three kick Patrick even harder as he keeps the deposit bag closer to him. The First Burglar pulls out a silver-gray jackknife.

Mrs. Howard, on her way home from shopping, sees the scene and SCREAMS OUT.

> MRS. HOWARD
> Oh, God! Help! They are killing a man
> here! Someone, call the police!

The First Burglar hides the deposit bag under his coat. He gestures at his gang "Let's split!" and then runs away.

The SECOND BURGLAR, a thin figure, pushes Mrs. Howard down and then runs away.

The Forth Burglar repeatedly kicks Patrick's waist. The THIRD BURGLAR, a bulky figure, yanks the Forth Burglar away, and they flee together.

Patrick GROANS on the ground.

MRS. HOWARD
You'll be fine, Mister Marlow! I'm now
calling an ambulance!

PATRICK
No… Please… Call Frankenstein…

Patrick points to the snowdrop flower. Mrs. Howard finds Patrick's cellphone in the flowerpot. She looks through the contact list and finally finds "Frankenstein."

EXT. ALLEY#1 – DAY

The First Burglar dashes into the alley. He sees a fire truck and a police car near a half-burned house. He slows down, turns around, and heads for the next alley. Cops are after him because of his suspicious behavior.

EXT. ALLEY#2 – DAY

While walking down the alley, the First Burglar notices two cops chasing him. He gestures, "What's the problem?", then calmly raises his hands. A cop frisks him but finds nothing suspicious. He then swiftly removes his ski mask. We DON'T SEE the First Burglar's face.

EXT. STREET#1 – DAY

The Second Burglar runs at full speed towards the bus shelter and leaps onto the bus at the last moment, taking off his ski mask. We DON'T SEE the Second Burglar's face.

EXT. ALLEY#3 – DAY

While running away, the Third and Fourth Burglars notice a worn building with its door open and they rush inside.

INT. VINTAGE ELEVATOR – DAY

The Third and Fourth Burglars hide inside the elevator, which has an "OUT OF ORDER" sign on its door. They remove their ski masks, out of breath. We DON'T SEE their faces.

EXT. MAIN STREET – DAY

An ambulance struggles to find its way through heavy traffic as some cars are illegally using the emergency lane.

FLASHBACK: INT. LOBBY, TEXTILE COMPANY – DAY

The elevator doors open. Arthur exits, carrying a big gourmet gift basket. Four Italians in elegant suits, in their late thirties, follow him. MARCO is a tall man, FABIO is a bulky man, SERGIO is a thin man, and ROMINA is a short woman. Nancy bows respectfully. Jessica, in a lilac dress, greets them candidly and shakes their hands.

> JESSICA
> *Benvenuto a tutti*! How wonderful to
> see everyone again! Romina, Sergio,
> Fabio, Marco! Welcome back!

> SERGIO
> *Ciao*, Jessica! Thank you!

> ROMINA
> *Grazie*, Jessica! It's been a long time!

> FABIO
> Almost a year! *Mamma Mia*!

Marco kisses Jessica's hand, his attention fixed on her engagement ring.

> MARCO
> We are truly happy to be back here,
> Jessica. This feels like home.

JESSICA
Lovely to hear this, Marco, thank you.
So, let's start with a drink, huh? Who
is thirsty?

MARCO
We are all thirsty for your exceptional
hospitality.

While Italians enter the cocktail lounge, Arthur whispers in Jessica's ear about Marco.

ARTHUR
He still looks fabulous, huh?

JESSICA
Give me a break, Arthur!

ARTHUR
Come on, don't be so short- tempered.
I'm not comparing. We know that no one
is ever as fabulous as Oliver! *Mamma mia!*

Jessica smiles as she enters the lounge. Arthur, tired from carrying the basket, follows her.

INT. OLIVER'S OFFICE – DAY

Oliver, in a black suit, searches his messy desk for something. He then makes an internal call.

OLIVER
Hey, couldn't you guys find him yet?
I'm sick of waiting here!

Bryan approaches Oliver's office, dragging a large plastic cover.

OLIVER (CON'T)
Never mind! Just showed up!

                    BRYAN
          Were you looking for me, boss?

                    OLIVER
          Where the hell have you been?

Bryan examines the plastic cover against the door to see if it is large
enough to cover it.

                    BRYAN
          In the storeroom. Looking for something
          to cover your door until it's fixed.

                    OLIVER
          Well, it's time to put your "hide-and-
          seek" skills to the test, Bryan. I can't
          find the goddamn statistics file!

Bryan shifts one or two papers and finds the file.

                    BRYAN
          You mean this one?

                    OLIVER
          I have no idea how you are doing this!
          Thanks, man!

                    BRYAN
          I have magical hands, boss. And now
          they'll find sticky tape to secure this
          magical cover to your door, and it will
          protect you from our big boss's big eyes.

                    OLIVER
          That's an offer I can't refuse.

Oliver CHUCKLES. He then notices the scar on Bryan's brow.

                    OLIVER
          Hey, is that a scar?

> BRYAN

Yeah, I've just bumped my head in the storeroom. It's a complete mess down there, boss, I'm telling you. Oh, I forgot the sticky tape.

Bryan exits. Oliver answers his RINGING cellphone.

> OLIVER

Hey, Doc, what a surprise! Or are you finally ready to say goodbye to that shabby car?
> (jumps to his feet)

What? Oh, my God! But he is fine, right? Please, take good care of him, Doc! I'm on my way!

He rushes out while Bryan approaches with sticky tape.

> BRYAN

Hey, why the rush, boss?

> OLIVER

My dad was attacked by thieves!

Oliver storms out of the building.

> BRYAN
> (baffled)

What?

INT. LOBBY, TEXTILE COMPANY – DAY

Nancy picks up the RINGING desk phone.

> NANCY

Crodney Textiles, good afternoon! Oh, hello again, Mister Marlow. What? Oh, my goodness! Yes, of course, I'll inform her right away. I hope your father recovers soon.

Nancy hangs up the phone, takes timid steps, and glances inside the lounge.

Italians and Arthur are conversing while tasting their cocktails. While Jessica, in a black dress, sipping her water, notices Nancy and gives her a dark stare. Nancy rushes back to her desk as she is having cold feet.

INT. DOCTOR'S OFFICE, HOSPITAL – DAY

DOCTOR FRANCISCO, 55, a respectable Korean doctor, is analyzing a medical report at his desk. Oliver, in a black suit, is nervously tapping his cellphone on his knee.

> OLIVER
> Doc, are you planning to tell me what
> I'm waiting for?

The Doctor sighs, then leaves the report on the desk.

> DOCTOR FRANCISCO
> Sorry, Oliver. I needed to double-check
> these reports first.

> OLIVER
> I don't care about your reports, Doc! I'm
> here to see my father! I need to be sure
> he is okay!

> DOCTOR FRANCISCO
> All the necessary treatments were given
> to him in no time, Oliver. Be a little patient.
> You'll see him as soon as he is taken to his
> private room.

> OLIVER
> Why, where is he now?

> DOCTOR FRANCISCO
> There're a few more procedures to be completed.
> That's why he was taken upstairs after the dialysis.

OLIVER
Dialysis? Why on earth he needs a
dialyzer?

DOCTOR FRANCISCO
Because of two unpleasant reasons I
have to share with you. Firstly, during
his examination, an atrophic kidney case
was discovered on the right-hand side.

OLIVER
Wait, wait, atro-what?

The Doctor holds two note papers - one in each hand.

DOCTOR FRANCISCO
Atrophic. It means that his right kidney
has not been working at all.

The Doctor crumples the notepaper in his right hand.

OLIVER
At all? But my father never mentioned
that before.

DOCTOR FRANCISCO
He was probably unaware of it. And I
believe we both know why.

OLIVER
Yeah! Because he is scared shitless of
doctors, hospitals, medical tests, and
everything related to them! Shit!

Oliver punches the wall while pacing back and forth.

DOCTOR FRANCISCO
Atrophic means a shrinkage in the size
of the kidney. The thing is, if one of your
kidneys is functioning properly, you may
never know that the other one is atrophic.

OLIVER
Why this kind of thing happens?

DOCTOR FRANCISCO
Might be various reasons, such as a
renal artery blockage or a urinary
system obstruction. It may even be
innate. Many people around the world
are living just like that, without a clue.

OLIVER
But there should be some treatment
methods for this! It's the twenty-first
century, for God's sake!

DOCTOR FRANCISCO
There is, but the journey is not so lovable.
And if we come to think about Patrick's
age, the process won't get any shorter.
Plus, some side effects may appear, most
likely in his respiratory system. Breathing
problems, you can say.

OLIVER
So, he has to hang in there with the left
one until the other one heals.

DOCTOR FRANCISCO
Apparently, he was already doing so.
Until today.

The Doctor crumples the notepaper in his hand.

OLIVER
"Until today?" What do you mean?

DOCTOR FRANCISCO
And here comes the second one. Oliver, your father was definitely not in good condition when he arrived here. He was apparently swiped in the nephritic area. Badly. And mostly on his left side. And it seems that the time he'd lost on the way here worsened the situation.

OLIVER
Those bastards! Why don't they just bug off after taking the damn money, huh? I will smite those psychopaths with my own hands!

DOCTOR FRANCISCO
The official investigation is in progress, Oliver. Just as it should be. Can you please take a seat for a moment? We need to discuss how to overcome this problem, right now. Eventually, time is the ultimate luxury in life, right?

Oliver sighs in frustration and sits down.

OLIVER
Okay, Doc, okay, you are right. I'm listening.

DOCTOR FRANCISCO
Good. Now, here is the deal. The aggressive beatings took a toll on his left kidney, causing it to lose all of its functions and creating a severe infection around the organ. So, it has to be removed right away.

The Doctor throws the crumpled paper in his hand.

OLIVER
You mean...

DOCTOR FRANCISCO
Yes, Oliver. Your father requires a kidney
transplant. Immediately.

OLIVER
Oh, my God! So, when will you do that?

DOCTOR FRANCISCO
Frankly speaking, we need to get him to
surgery in the shortest possible time if we
are lucky enough to find a kidney for him.

Oliver rises to his feet and removes his jacket.

OLIVER
So, take mine, Doc! Stop chewing the rag
and take my kidney! Come on, I am ready
to be cut here!

DOCTOR FRANCISCO
Good to know that, Oliver, but it's not quite
that simple. The kidney should be compatible,
and I'm afraid yours are not.

OLIVER
Well, how do you know that, Doc? From the
hour-long gawky look on my face or from
my magical ass-print on that couch?

DOCTOR FRANCISCO
Neither.

The Doctor grabs the medical report that he was analyzing at the
beginning of the conversation.

DOCTOR FRANCISCO (CON'T)
Before starting the process, a cross-matching
test must be performed to analyze the patient's
and donor's test results. You might've forgotten,
Oliver, but I have your annual check-up results.
And here is your cross-matching chart.

> OLIVER
> So, what does it say?

> DOCTOR FRANCISCO
> It says "incompatible!"

> OLIVER
> What? That's not possible, Doc. You
> need to double-check it.

> DOCTOR FRANCISCO
> I did.

> OLIVER
> You did, and this is the final result, huh?
> (kicks the wall)
> Misfortunes never come alone!

> DOCTOR FRANCISCO
> I also would like to mention that the walls
> have recently been painted, Oliver.

Oliver notices the stain on the white wall that he caused.

> DOCTOR FRANCISCO (CON'T)
> Trying to solve a problem by creating a
> new one is not a pretty smart idea, Oliver.
> Just keep that in mind for the future. Wait
> here. I'll be right back.

The Doctor grabs the folder and exits. Oliver tries to remove the stain from the wall, but he only makes it worse. He drags a chair to hide it.

INT. LOBBY, TEXTILE COMPANY – DAY

Jessica, in a black dress, the Italians, and Arthur emerge from the lounge and approach the conference room. Nancy gathers her courage and approaches Jessica.

NANCY
Miss Bayley, I have to inform you about--

JESSICA
I don't want to hear it unless it's about
a giant meteor approaching the Earth
right now!

Nancy can't say a word.

JESSICA (CON'T)
Is it?

Nancy shakes her head no. Jessica goes into the conference room. Nancy feels hopeless. The "NO!" paper in Jessica's office catches her eye. Nancy goes to her desk and begins to write a note to Jessica.

INT. CAR SHOWROOM – DAY

Bryan is on the phone, surrounded by coworkers.

EMPLOYEES
We are all praying for him, boss! We are
with you!

BRYAN
Do you hear them? Never let anything
gets you down, boss! Be always positive!

INT. FLOOR#3, HOSPITAL – DAY

Oliver is seated on a bench near Room#303, talking on his cellphone.

OLIVER
What are you talking about, Bryan? I'm
almost gonna punch myself in the face
here! I am the reason my father is
suffering in this damn hospital right now!

A YOUNG COUPLE enter Room#303 to visit a patient. Their 5-year-old daughter, LILY, holds a fancy ceramic flowerpot. Many other visitors and bouquets can be seen in the room.

> OLIVER (CON'T)
> He wanted to visit me at work today,
> but what I did? I sent him into the
> middle of the violence just like that!
> He now needs a new kidney, and we
> don't have much time to find one.

Oliver gets irritated by the noisy visitors in Room#303. Their shrieking kids munch biscuits and chase each other. Oliver motions to NURSE WENDY, 28, asking her warn them. Nurse Wendy rolls her eyes and heads for the room.

INT. ROOM#303, HOSPITAL – DAY

Visitors assist a MALE PATIENT, 50, with wearing his shirt. Kids place biscuits on the windowsill, hoping for some pigeons to land. Nurse Wendy appears in the doorway.

> NURSE WENDY
> Hey, folks, what if you keep it down, huh?
> We receive complaints!

> MALE PATIENT
> Oh, sorry, Nurse. We just got some good
> news. That's why.

> NURSE WENDY
> You want more news? Those flowers are
> not allowed here! This is not a cemetery!
> Pollens can easily cause allergic reactions
> in other patients, which means much more
> work for us, right?

> VISITOR MAN
> Yes, Miss, don't worry. We'll get rid of them
> all right away.

When Lily hears this, she grabs the fancy ceramic flowerpot and conceals it on the windowsill's outer corner without being noticed.

                              MALE PATIENT
               I've already been released. We are about
               to leave the hospital.

                              NURSE WENDY
          Great news!

Nurse Wendy exits the room, SLAMMING the door behind her.

INT. FLOOR#3, HOSPITAL – DAY

Oliver jumps to his feet when he sees the caregivers bringing Patrick on a stretcher. He holds Patrick's hand. Patrick tries to hide his pain behind a smile. Along with the stretcher, Oliver enters Room#301.

The male patient and his visitors exit Room#303. Lily cries to take her flowerpot, but her parents firmly hold her hands as they walk down the stairs.

INT. LOBBY, TEXTILE COMPANY – DAY

The Italians and Arthur exit the conference room and enter the elevator. Marco prefers to wait for Jessica. Jessica goes to her office to take her belongings. She finds the note, reads it, and approaches Nancy's desk.

                              JESSICA
               An assault with the intent to rob, huh?

                              NANCY
          I am really sorry, Miss Bayley.

                              JESSICA
               He is now using his father to trick me?
               Shameless!

NANCY
What? You think he is lying? But he
sounded really worried.

JESSICA
Being believable. It's the foremost
characteristic of professional liars.
However, they are not very talented
at "building a good story."

Arthur calls out to her from the elevator.

ARTHUR
Come on, Jessica! Do you want us to
starve in this metal box?

Jessica crumples the notepaper and puts it in Nancy's hand. Nancy is
confused. Jessica steps into the elevator. Marco follows her in, and the
elevator doors close.

INT. DOCTOR'S OFFICE, HOSPITAL – DAY

Doctor Francisco is on the phone.

DOCTOR FRANCISCO
I know there is a waiting list, my friend.
Patrick is already in it, but we are out
of time here. Frankly speaking, I have
no idea how he's still hanging in there.

The Doctor notices the black jacket on the ground that's thrown down
by Oliver earlier that day. He grabs and hangs it on the coat rack.

DOCTOR FRANCISCO (CON'T)
No, A.B.O. is not a solution for us. It takes
weeks to complete. No, my friend, I'm
simply asking you quickly check if there
is any donation with no demand. Yes,
it's AB-positive.

He regains hope and sits at his computer.

> DOCTOR FRANCISCO (CON'T)
> You will? I knew I could count on you,
> my friend! Tell me your email address!

INT. ROOM#301, HOSPITAL – DAY

Patrick leans back on his bed. NURSE ANDREA, 23, examines his medical chart. The Brunette Officer takes Patrick's testimony. The Blonde Officer takes notes.

> BRUNETTE OFFICER
> Well, thanks for the information you
> provided, Mister Marlow.

> BLONDE OFFICER
> It was not much though. If you will
> remember something else--

> PATRICK
> I don't think that I can!

> BLONDE OFFICER
> You mean, because of the medications
> you were given?

> PATRICK
> No! Because I've already told you
> everything! I've lost my kidney, not
> my memory!

Patrick coughs. Oliver brings him a glass of water.

> OLIVER
> Dad, are you okay?

> PATRICK
> I am tired of being treated like a parrot
> here!

                    NURSE ANDREA
Excuse me, officers, but Mister Marlow
has already had a rough day. He needs
to rest now.

The Blonde Officer hands the business card to Oliver.

                    BLONDE OFFICER
Here. Just in case.

                    OLIVER
Thank you, officers. No doubt that you
will catch those monsters in no time.

The two officers bow and exit.

                    NURSE ANDREA
Try not to drink too much water, Mister
Marlow. And if you require assistance,
press the red button.

                    OLIVER
Thank you, Nurse Andrea. I hope we
won't need it at all.

Nurse Andrea exits the room with a sincere smile.

                    PATRICK
Go get her, son!

                    OLIVER
What, dad, you have pain?

                    PATRICK
Not the nurse, you lanky chicken!
Go get Jessica!

                    OLIVER
Dad, it's not the time. You heard the nurse.
You need to get rest. Do not think about
anything, okay?

PATRICK
Do you know what the most famous
side effect of resting is?

OLIVER
No, what?

PATRICK
Thinking!

OLIVER
Dad…

PATRICK
(imploringly)
Son… Please… Go, get her here. Consider
this to be my last will.

OLIVER
Dad, please, stop doing this. We'll soon
find the best kidney for you, and you
will be fine.

PATRICK
I'll be fine once I see you two love birds
happy again… right here… next to my
sickbed… with my grandkids…

Patrick wipes his small tears with the back of his hand.

OLIVER
With your grandkids? Dad, are you aware
how weird and illogical you sound right
now?

PATRICK
Life is too magical to be logical, son! You've
had three decades to figure this out!

OLIVER
Okay, enough of talking.

                    PATRICK
          I haven't even started yet!

Patrick sniffs. Oliver brings him a tissue box.

                    OLIVER
          I told you a hundred times that she
          didn't respond to my calls.

                    PATRICK
          So what? In our time, we used to be
          able to communicate with each other
          without dialing some stupid numbers!

                    OLIVER
          Her office is on the other end of the city.
          Even if I drove there, it would take hours,
          and I don't want to leave you here alone
          for that long.

                    PATRICK
          That's okay, son. I assure you that I'll be
          waiting right here, ignoring all kinds of
          invitations.

                    OLIVER
          What invitations?

                    PATRICK
          From heaven or hell... Who knows?...

                    OLIVER
                (out of patience)
          Oh, God!

                    PATRICK
          Yeah, he might know.

Oliver paces around, then looks at Patrick's bleary eyes.

OLIVER
Okay, dad, you win. I'll go get her.

PATRICK
Now you are talking! You don't need to
be worried about me, son. Frankenstein
will look after me.

Doctor Francisco enters the room.

PATRICK
A-ha! Speak of the devil!

OLIVER
Dad…

DOCTOR FRANCISCO
That's okay, Oliver. After all, he is our
most distinguished guest here. He only
comes to visit us every sixty years or so.

OLIVER
Yeah, tell me about it. So, as per a strict
order from a strict man, it's time for me
to hit the road!

PATRICK
Have a memorable journey, son!

Oliver kisses Patrick on the forehead and thankfully taps the Doctor on
the shoulder, then exits. The Doctor sits.

DOCTOR FRANCISCO
So, how are you feeling so far?

PATRICK
Like a shriveled vegetable!

DOCTOR FRANCISCO
Everything will work out for the best,
Patrick. You know that, right?

                    PATRICK
         I know, Frankie. I know.

Nurse Andrea KNOCKS on the open door.

                    NURSE ANDREA
         Doctor Francisco, sorry to interrupt, but
         the girl in 215 has locked herself in the
         bathroom! She is again forcing herself to
         vomit! And Mister Cobb is still insisting on
         to go home! He shattered yet another lamp!

                    DOCTOR FRANCISCO
         What about the monitor?

                    NURSE ANDREA
         No, it's fine. We had already covered it
         with a blanket.

                    DOCTOR FRANCISCO
         That's my team! Thanks, Andrea. I'll be
         with you in a minute.
                    (to Patrick)
         It's time for me to bounce from room to
         room. Relax and take a nap, okay? I'll be
         around.

The Doctor exits. Patrick sinks into sleep in no time.

INT. FOYER, BASEMENT APARTMENT – DAY

IVY, 22, a short girl with old red boots, is ready to go out, waiting for
her boyfriend who is in the bathroom.

                    IVY
         Nicolas! Hurry up, darling! I don't want
         to miss the damn bus!

Ivy notices a cockroach crawling around the foyer. She tramples on it
and simply throws it out.

INT. BATHROOM, BASEMENT APARTMENT – DAY

NICOLAS, 30, a bulky young man, combs his hair while talking on his cellphone under his breath.

> NICOLAS
> Oh, no! Ivy is getting upset, bro! I have
> to go. Listen. I want everything tonight
> to be perfect in every way, okay?
> Flowers, candles, everything.

He takes the golden ring from its pouch. It's engraved with the names "IVY & NICOLAS."

> NICOLAS (CON'T)
> You are the best bro ever! By the way,
> Hector, you guys will never ever let her
> notice, okay? About what? The secrets
> of the pyramids! No, bro! About my
> proposal, of course!

EXT. GROCERY – DAY

HECTOR, 32, a thin man with a hook-shaped tattoo on his neck, is on the phone. A GROCER prepares an onion bag.

> HECTOR
> Oh, that? Don't worry, bro. My lips are
> sealed. Just relax. You guys will find a
> smashing dinner table when you get
> back home.

The Grocer hands him the bag, but Hector can't hold it properly. Onions scatter everywhere.

INT. FOYER, BASEMENT APARTMENT – DAY

Nicolas emerges from the bathroom and kisses Ivy.

                    NICOLAS
          I'm ready, darling. Let's go.

                      IVY
          Finally! But, darling, you'll catch a cold
          like this, come on!

Ivy buttons up Nicolas' dull coat to protect his neck.

                    NICOLAS
          You are my angel.

Ivy intensely smells his neck.

                      IVY
          You are my oxygen.

EXT. PARKING LOT – DAY

Hundreds of cars are parked. While waiting in line at the ticket counter, Charles gives himself a head massage. He pays the fee. The Attendant points to a distant section of the parking lot. While heading for his yellowish jalopy, Charles answers his RINGING cellphone.

                    CHARLES
          Nicolas, what's up? Yeah, I've finally
          found it at the end of nowhere!

Charles pretends to take a puff on his unlit cigarette.

                    CHARLES (CON'T)
          I also had to pay for the towing service
          and the parking fee! Can you believe this
          bullshit? No, but I'll look into it right away.
          Even if a single matchstick is missing from
          that car, these guys are in big trouble.
          Where are you now? Okay. Then I'll pick
          you up first and we will drive there together.
          Sounds good?

EXT. BUS SHELTER – DAY

As the public bus moves away, Ivy blows a kiss to Nicolas from behind the bus window. Nicolas smiles and waves at Ivy from the bus shelter while talking on his cellphone.

> NICOLAS
> Yeah, but hurry up, Charles. There is a
> lot more work to be done for me today,
> you know. It's the big day for my sweet
> princess and me.

INTERCUT WITH CHARLES IN THE PARKING LOT:

Charles pops the trunk of his yellowish jalopy and looks through the big plastic bags while on the phone.

> CHARLES
> You are an incurable romantic, man!
> Anyway… Surprisingly, everything
> seems in order here. You wait there.
> I'm on my way.

The unlit cigarette slips from his lips and lands on the ground. Charles closes the trunk, then bends down to pick it up. He notices a kitten hiding upon the wheel.

He makes an effort to save the kitten and then puts it beneath a tree. He gets in his car and tries to start the stubborn engine for a while. It finally starts.

As the yellowish jalopy moves away, a wet spot on the ground comes in sight.

LIGHTNINGS CRACK in the cloudy sky.

INT. OLIVER'S CAR – DAY

Oliver drives through a DOWNHILL ROAD towards the CROSSROADS, talking on his cellphone through earbuds.

> OLIVER
>
> I am sorry to hear that, cousin. I had no
> idea you were diabetic. No, of course, in
> this case, you are unable to donate kidneys.

When the car hits a pothole, Oliver loses control and quickly regains it.

> OLIVER (CON'T)
>
> Shit! Oh, no, not to you, cousin. I just
> didn't notice the bloody chuckhole!

EXT. CROSSROADS – DAY

Oliver's car stops at the red lights. Oliver is unaware that the gas tank cracked at the time of the impact, causing gasoline to flow down towards the CROSSROADS. The driver in the next car is casually flicking a lighter.

INT. ROOM#301, HOSPITAL – DAY

Patrick awakens, GASPING for breath. He presses the red button. Nurse Andrea rushes inside. She removes one of the pillows from under Patrick's head to ease his airway. She quickly prepares an oxygen device.

> NURSE ANDREA
>
> Hang on, Mister Marlow! I'll make you
> breathe again! Please, hang on!

INT. OLIVER'S CAR – DAY

As the lights at the CROSSROADS turn green, Oliver drives away while talking on the phone through earbuds.

> OLIVER
>
> No, Katy can't donate, either. Well,
> apparently, she is 8-weeks pregnant.
> Yeah, after five years, it's a true miracle!

As he sees the traffic jam ahead, he flees into an alley.

INT. ROOM#301, HOSPITAL – DAY

Caregivers transfer Patrick from his bed to a stretcher. Nurse Andrea holds his oxygen mask. Doctor Francisco holds the door open for them to exit.

> DOCTOR FRANCISCO
> Intensive Care Unit! Hurry!

EXT. FLEA MARKET – DAY

A female stallholder, MARY, 55, eats snacks. Ivy approaches her stall and casually rubs the woolen jerseys.

> MARY
> They're as soft as silk, aren't they? And
> each one has a unique design. They're
> all knitted by a very talented lady.

Ivy smirks sarcastically.

> MARY (CON'T)
> Oh, no, not me. Sofia is her name. And
> I'm Mary.

> IVY
> So, Mary, you only have these?

> MARY
> No, I have many more in these boxes.
> Tell me what you need.

INT. YELLOWISH JALOPY – DAY

Charles drives through the DOWNHILL ROAD. He notices the pothole and makes the maneuver right on time.

                    CHARLES
          What the hell!

The unlit cigarette between his lips falls. Charles stops at the red lights on the CROSSROADS near the subway station, where Oliver stopped a few minutes ago. He is unaware of the gasoline river under his car. When he bends down to pick up his cigarette, the engine cuts out.

                    CHARLES
          No, shit! Not now!

A driver in the passing lane throws a cigarette butt out onto the road. It ignites the gasoline stream, and the blaze quickly reaches the yellowish jalopy. Charles is unaware of the fire under his car as he is trying to restart the engine. HORNS BLARE in order to warn him about the danger, but Charles is completely focused on the starter switch.

                    CHARLES
          Okay, okay! I know the green is on,
          you noisy buggers!

Charles repeatedly declutches and turns the key. Just as the engine starts, the car EXPLODES.

EXT. CROSSROADS – DAY

A MASSIVE CLOUD of SMOKE. Burning pieces of Charles's coat flit around the street.

INT. ROOM#401, HOSPITAL – DAY

Patrick, who is wearing an oxygen mask, TAKES a DEEP BREATH in his SLEEP and then resumes regular breathing.

EXT. FLEA MARKET – DAY

While Mary displays a bunch of different jerseys, Ivy makes a call to Nicolas.

> IVY
>
> Hey, darling, pick a color. Nothing.
> Come on, darling, just tell me one
> color and hush.

EXT. BUS SHELTER – DAY

Nicolas strolls around, talking on his cellphone.

> NICOLAS
>
> Then I'll say "dark blue." Are you happy
> now? No, darling, I'm stuck here, waiting
> for Charles. He will be here any second
> now, don't worry. I miss you already.
> See you in a few hours, darling.

EXT. FLEA MARKET – DAY

Ivy hangs up the phone and turns to Mary.

> IVY
>
> I need one in dark blue.

> MARY
>
> Oh, sure, sure, right here!

Mary displays a light-blue V- neck jersey.

> IVY
>
> Are you deaf or what? I said, "dark
> blue!" And it's better to be a turtleneck!

> MARY
>
> Oh, sure, hold on a second.

Mary searches in cardboard boxes.

INT. OLIVER'S CAR – DAY

Oliver drives down a silent alley, talking on his cellphone through earbuds.

                    OLIVER
          Yes, Officer, I understand what you are
          saying. No, I have no new information
          to share with you. I was just hoping to
          hear some good news. Sure, it's not a
          child's play. I wish you all good luck
          then, Officer. Sorry to bother. Bye.

Oliver is baffled as his car stutters. He sees that the fuel gauge is FLASHING RED.

                    OLIVER
          You've got to be kidding me!

The engine shuts down. Oliver is unable to restart it. Thick STEAM begins to emerge from the car's hood.

INT. KITCHEN, DANIEL'S APARTMENT – DAY

ROADWORK is barely HEARD. Daniel and Elliot are sitting at the lunch table. SOFIA, 45, at the kitchen counter, clumsily pours tomato soup into two bowls.

                    SOFIA
          Your father has every reason to get
          mad, dear. What if you break your
          arm or leg? God forbid!

Sofia serves them their soup bowls, then wipes the soup drops on the kitchen counter with a white rag.

                    DANIEL
          He now gets it very well, Sofia. No
          bicycle until the end of the school
          year! Right, Elliot?

Elliot slowly eats his soup.

> ELLIOT
>
> Yes, dad...

Daniel answers his RINGING cellphone, his mouth full.

> DANIEL
>
> Oliver, how is it going? What? Okay,
> okay, stop jabbering and send me
> your exact location. I'll try my best.

INTERCUT WITH OLIVER IN THE SILENT ALLEY:

The car's hood is open. After sending a message, Oliver hangs up his cellphone. He looks at the surrounding ambiance. He feels himself like an outsider.

A sharp CLAP of THUNDER.

INT. KITCHEN, DANIEL'S APARTMENT – DAY

Sofia fills a washbowl with water and rubs the white rag in it to remove the soup stains. It appears that this won't be an easy task.

A MESSAGE TONE is HEARD. Daniel checks his phone and heads for the door, still munching on a bread roll. None of them is aware that his wallet has fallen from his coverall's back pocket and landed on his chair.

> SOFIA
>
> Daniel, you haven't eaten anything yet.

> DANIEL
>
> Business before pleasure, Sofia.

Daniel exits the apartment. Elliot runs into his room while taking off his green jersey.

                    SOFIA
          Elliot! Where are you going, dear?
          Come back here! Finish your lunch!

Sofia opens a bleach bottle. While pouring bleach in the washbowl, she sees Daniel's wallet on the chair. She grabs it, opens the window, and sees Daniel exiting the building. Sofia is unable to make herself heard because of the ROADWORK, so she reflexively throws the bottle cap towards his head. Daniel sees her and catches the wallet.

Sofia returns to the sink. As there is no cap for the bleach bottle anymore, she transfers the bleach into a small water bottle and closes it. Her phone RINGS in another room.

INT. LIVING ROOM, DANIEL'S APARTMENT – DAY

There is a half-knit white scarf on the couch. Sofia rushes into the room and picks up her RINGING cellphone.

                    SOFIA
          Hello, Mary. No, that's fine. Tell me what
          you need. Yes, I think I had one. Wait.

Sofia checks the closet that is full of woolen jerseys. Elliot, in a red coat, appears in the doorway just for a second.

                    ELLIOT
          Mom, I am going out!

                    SOFIA
          Elliot! Your father will burst with
          anger; I am telling you!

INT. KITCHEN, DANIEL'S APARTMENT – DAY

Elliot takes a chocolate bar from the fridge. He notices the water bottle on the countertop and grabs it as well. He is unaware that it's full of bleach.

INT. LIVING ROOM, DANIEL'S APARTMENT – DAY

Sofia pouts when she hears the apartment door SLAM. She finally finds a dark blue turtleneck while on the phone.

> SOFIA
> I found one, Mary. Yes, it's dark blue.
> Oh, I see. Yes, sure, I can bring it myself
> if it's that urgent. Okay, see you soon.

Sofia grabs her stuff and exits the apartment in a hurry.

EXT. FLEA MARKET – DAY

Mary hangs up the phone and smiles at Ivy.

> MARY
> Good news! She is on the way with
> the turtleneck. It won't take long.

> IVY
> Better not!

INT. AUTO REPAIR SHOP – DAY

The pink car is already repaired and washed. The Apprentice is still working on the gray one. Elliot rushes into the shop, finds the keys in a drawer, unlocks the storeroom, and takes his bicycle out. He winks at the Apprentice while happily riding away.

INT. INTENSIVE CARE UNIT HALLWAY, HOSPITAL – DAY

Doctor Francisco is on his cellphone.

> DOCTOR FRANCISCO
> Yes, he is in the Intensive Care Unit, but
> he is fine. This is the standard procedure,
> Oliver, as I explained to you twice before.

He looks through the glass wall at Patrick, who is asleep.

                    DOCTOR FRANCISCO (CON'T)
          Don't worry, I've got my eye on him. No.
          Still no news about the kidney. I'll call
          you when we find one. Of course, we will.
          There is no other option, Oliver.

EXT. SILENT ALLEY – DAY

Oliver is talking on his cellphone in his still car as the rain pours down
outside.

                    OLIVER
          Please, keep my father alive, Doc. Please.

Oliver hangs up. He feels desperate. He sees an approaching tow truck
– Daniel and a driver inside. As Daniel exits, Oliver exits as well.

                    OLIVER
          Daniel, thank God you are here!

                    DANIEL
          We had to turn around all the way
          down from the artery. The road was
          reduced to one lane up there.

                    OLIVER
          Better late than never. We'll talk the
          details later, okay? I need to dash for
          the subway.

Oliver dashes eastward.

                    DANIEL
          Forget it, Oliver! The subway entrance
          is also closed!

                    OLIVER
          What? Why?

DANIEL
Who can tell? There might be a massive
car accident or something! You'd better
try hailing a taxi!

Oliver waves at him thankfully while dashing westward.

INT. ELEGANT RESTAURANT – DAY

Jessica, in a black dress, the Italians, and Arthur are sitting at an elaborate table, checking the menus.

Jessica sees a happy couple with their cute baby having lunch at another table. She sadly bites into a bread roll and stares out at the view. Marco sips his wine; his gaze is drawn to the ring mark on Jessica's finger.

MARCO
Jessica?... Jessica?...

JESSICA
Oh, sorry, Marco, did you say something?

MARCO
Only your name. I had no idea you were
so deeply in love, Jessica.
(off her puzzled look)
With this lovely city, I mean. You can't
take your eyes off of it.

JESSICA
Well, despite the fact that it's a huge
backbreaker, I believe that you are
correct, Marco.

MARCO
It's worth the effort as far as the love
is concerned. Am I right?

Instead of responding, Jessica takes a sip of her water.

MARCO (CON'T)
Don't you think so, Arthur?

ARTHUR
(focused on the menu)
Yeah, they all look delicious!

Italians LAUGH at him. Jessica forces a smile.

EXT. BUS SHELTER – DAY

Nicolas is sick of waiting. He makes a call to Charles.

RECORDED VOICE (V.O.)
The person you have called--

NICOLAS
Vanished into thin air!

Meanwhile, across the street, Elliot rides his bicycle towards a dog and HONKS, causing the dog to jump into the street. To save the dog, a DRIVER turns the wheel, but he hits Nicolas at the bus shelter. People gather around him, including the Bearded Old Man and a YOUNG GIRL.

Elliot crosses the street, leans his bike against a tree, and pushes his way through the crowd to see the scene. Nicolas is writhing in agony on the sidewalk.

ELLIOT
My god! Is he okay? He is gonna live,
right?

BEARDED OLD MAN
His leg seems crooked.

ELLIOT
Oh no! And his head is bleeding! I'll go
find a pharmacy!

Elliot rushes away. The Young Girl speaks up.

                    YOUNG GIRL
          Okay, folks, I've just made the call!
          The ambulance is on its way!

                    BEARDED OLD MAN
          Some water may help him feel better
          until they arrive.

The Bearded Old Man grabs the water bottle from Elliot's bike basket and makes Nicolas drink some water. Nicolas refuses to drink more, coughing badly.

                    YOUNG GIRL
          Wait a minute! What is that?

She grabs and smells the bottle.

                    YOUNG GIRL (CON'T)
          Hey, this is not water! This is bleach!

                    BEARDED OLD MAN
                 (puzzled)
          What? Are you sure?

                    YOUNG GIRL
          You wanna taste some?

The Bearded Old Man barely smells the bottle.

                    BEARDED OLD MAN
          Good heavens! How dangerous is it?

                    YOUNG GIRL
          Not more than goodwill without awareness!

EXT. OLIVER'S BUILDING – DAY

It's lightly raining. Violet, in a good mood, walks towards the building, holding her purse over her hair bun.

A taxi pulls off the road. Oliver, drenched in rain, pays the taxi driver and asks him while exiting:

                    OLIVER
          Can you wait here for a minute?
          I'll be right back.

The driver nods yes. Oliver sees Violet. She is about to enter the building.

                    OLIVER
          Violet, wait!

                    VIOLET
          Oliver, hi! What's wrong?

                    OLIVER
          Nothing is in order, actually.

                    VIOLET
          Is it about your fiancée?

                    OLIVER
          Not only that. A lot has happened today,
          Violet. I need your help if your offer is
          still valid.

                    VIOLET
          Absolutely. I was going to have lunch
          with my aunt, but I can postpone it.
          Just tell me what I can do for you.

                    OLIVER
          I'm on my way to Jessica's office to
          properly explain everything. I'd be
          glad if you could come with me.
          You know, to back me up?

HORNS BLARE as Oliver's taxi blocks the lane.

> VIOLET
> Yes, of course. Allow me five seconds;
> I need to inform my aunt.

Violet communicates with her aunt via the building's intercom. Unexpectedly, a man enters Oliver's taxi, and it speeds away.

> OLIVER
> Hey, you said you'd wait! Shit!

Oliver tries to hail another taxi, but it splatters mud on him while passing.

Violet is saddened by Oliver's desperate look. Noticing another taxi approaching, she positions her purse beneath her jacket to appear pregnant and steps forward with a grimace. The taxi stops right away. Oliver is confused by the situation.

EXT. STREET# - DAY

It's lightly raining. Elliot and a PHARMACIST rush towards the bus shelter. They slow down when they see the crowd receding and an ambulance is moving away.

The Pharmacist heads back to work. Elliot sadly walks away, dragging his bicycle.

EXT. FLEA MARKET – DAY

Ivy and Mary converse beneath a tarpaulin.

> IVY
> And then I dropped out of Nursing School.

> MARY
> Oh, poor girl. You had given up your dreams
> for Nicolas, huh?

IVY
What dream? It was nothing but a
nightmare! I was going to that stupid
school only because of my evil father's
persistence! And the "nursing internship"
part was even more disgusting. I really
don't get why people don't just die directly
instead of occupying others with their misery!

Mary is bewildered.

IVY (CON'T)
So, one night, when I was nineteen, I packed
my bag and abandoned home without a trace.

MARY
Oh, I am sorry, dear.

IVY
I am not. I've been with Nicolas since then.
He is my breath of life!

MARY
I suppose, the dark-blue jersey will be a
gift for him.

IVY
You are smart, huh? Yeah, today is our
third dating anniversary.

An exhausted Sofia approaches them, holding an umbrella.

MARY
Oh, there she is!

IVY
Finally!

SOFIA
Sorry for keeping you waiting, ladies. But the
bus somehow took a different route today.

                    IVY
          Do I look like a bus inspector here?
          Just show me the jersey!

Sofia becomes bewildered. Just as she is about to show her the dark-blue turtleneck, Ivy's cellphone RINGS.

                    IVY (CON'T)
          Wait. Nicolas might have changed his
          mind about the color.

Sofia and Mary exchange a look. Ivy answers her phone.

                    IVY
          Hey, darling!
                    (perplexed)
          Yes, this is she! Who the hell are you?!
                    (terrified)
          What ambulance? What? No way! How
          is he? Hand him the phone! I am speaking
          to you, you idiot! I want to talk to Nicolas!

Mary and Sofia seem bewildered, watching Ivy rush away.

INT. AMBULANCE – DAY

The First Aid Team splint Nicolas' broken leg. While talking on Nicolas' cellphone, a FIRST AID NURSE dresses the wounds around his lips.

                    FIRST AID NURSE
          Please, calm down. Everything is under
          control here. No, it's better if we don't
          force him to speak right now. No, ma'am!
          You can see him at the hospital!

INT. AUTO REPAIR SHOP – DAY

The Apprentice is still working on the gray car.

A sad Elliot enters, drenched in rain. He locks his bicycle into the storeroom and then shuffles out of the shop.

INT. TAXI#1 – DAY

It's drizzling. MUSIC is barely HEARD on the radio. Behind the wheel is a GRUMPY TAXI DRIVER, 25. Violet sobs in the backseat. Oliver tries to calm her down.

> OLIVER
> Violet, please. It's not your fault that
> he was attacked.

> VIOLET
> How can you say that? If I hadn't ruined
> your relationship yesterday, your father
> would never go to that bank today!

> OLIVER
> But I am the one who put the question
> marks in his head. I should have explained
> to him the real reason for the breakup.

> VIOLET
> Yes, the reason I caused!

> OLIVER
> Hey, wait a minute. What are we doing
> here? You are blaming yourself. I am
> blaming myself. I even blamed my father
> for his hasty decision. But what about
> those heartless burglars, huh? I'm sure
> they are throwing a party right now!

> VIOLET
> I hope they reap what they sow!

The Grumpy Driver is sick of her sobbing. He tunes up the radio, driving over the London Bridge towards the east.

INT. KITCHEN, BASEMENT APARTMENT – DAY

Hector cooks while singing to himself. He doesn't mind the blackflies buzzing around. He takes a sip of his beer and pours some into the frypan. The chopped onions sizzle. Hector picks up his RINGING cellphone.

> HECTOR
> Ivy, what's up? Hey, are you crying?
> What? Oh, no! How is he now? How is he?

INT. TAXI#2 – DAY

It's drizzling. The taxi cruises over the London Bridge towards the west. Ivy is on her cellphone, crying.

> IVY
> The nurse said he was alright, but I
> have no reason to believe that bitch!
> Hurry up, Hector! Nicolas might need
> a blood transfusion or something!

INTERCUT WITH HECTOR IN THE KITCHEN:

Hector turns off the oven and storms out of the apartment, not even getting his coat, still talking on his cellphone.

> HECTOR
> Yeah, I'm now taking off! I'll call Charles
> as well!

INT. GLAZIERS' SHOP – DAY

After loading the cut window glass into the delivery car, the two glaziers return to the shop.

As the Short Glazier prepares to grab another piece of window glass, the Tall Glazier approaches a large piece of frosted glass.

> TALL GLAZIER
> Hey, leave it there, dude! Not ready yet.
> Let's grab this one!

> SHORT GLAZIER
> I thought these small ones were ordered
> before that frosted glass.

> TALL GLAZIER
> This is for the car showroom, dude! The
> guy will pay double! Come on, don't you
> wanna cheer up your wallet a little, huh?

They hold the large frosted glass, smirking.

EXT. BLIND ALLEY – DAY

It's raining. Hector rushes out of an old building, holding his cellphone against his ear. He races towards the street, nearly colliding with a lilac tree. He hangs up the phone and mutters to himself.

> HECTOR
> Where the hell are you, Charles?

EXT. GLAZIERS' SHOP – DAY

Hector speeds around the corner while the two glaziers carry the large frosted glass to the delivery car. There is not enough distance to slow down, so Hector crashes into the glass. It BREAKS down into SMITHEREENS, and a shard of glass severely cuts Hector's neck.

> TALL GLAZIER
> What the hell?!

With a blood-squirting throat, Hector gasps for breath on the sidewalk. The Tall Glazier applies pressure to stop the bleeding. The Short Glazier is paralyzed with fear.

> TALL GLAZIER (CON'T)
> Call someone, dude! The man is on his
> way to the graveyard here!

The Short Glazier drops his cellphone, panicking. Hector draws his last breath in the Tall Glazier's arms. Sparse raindrops disappear in the pool of blood.

INT. ROOM#401, HOSPITAL – DAY

Patrick, who is wearing an oxygen mask, TAKES a DEEP BREATH in his SLEEP and then resumes regular breathing.

INT. FLOOR#2, HOSPITAL – DAY

Doctor Francisco heads for the stairs, talking on his cellphone.

> DOCTOR FRANCISCO
> Anyway, I appreciate your effort, my friend.
> No, no. You know that I never give up hope
> in anything. I'm just getting a bit upset when
> I think of all those potential kidneys rotting
> away underground with no purpose.

He exchanges a polite nod with Nurse Wendy, who walks down the hallway with Ivy. The two women round a corner.

> IVY
> How is his condition now?

> NURSE WENDY
> He is sleeping with his leg in a cast.
> He won't be able to walk.

> IVY
> What?

> NURSE WENDY (CON'T)
> ...for at least six weeks.

                          IVY
          Oh, thank god!

Ivy gives her a stern look. This nurse talks in riddles just to mock people.

                          IVY (CON'T)
          I mean, for his narrow escape!

The two women pass by the laboratory, which has a sign on its door that reads, "AUTHORIZED PERSONNEL ONLY."

                          IVY (CON'T)
          And what about poisoning?

                          NURSE WENDY
          Drip-feeding will help him survive.

                          IVY
          I still don't get it. How come he drinks
          bleach?

                          NURSE WENDY
          It's a frequent case for us, but not for
          you guys, I guess.

                          IVY
          No! We usually drink hydrochloric acid!

Nurse Wendy boringly sighs and hands Ivy a sealed bag.

                          NURSE WENDY
          His personal belongings!

She then opens the door of Room#203.

                          NURSE WENDY (CON'T)
          And himself!

INT. ROOM#203, HOSPITAL – DAY

Nicolas is on a drip and fast asleep, with his leg in a cast. Ivy rushes inside and rubs his hair. She looks over his medical chart. Everything seems in order. She then cracks open the sealed bag to check his belongings.

> IVY
> Let's see. Keys, here. Cell phone, okay.
> Wallet, here...
>> (checking the wallet)
> Driving license, okay. Money okay,
> I suppose.

She curiously pulls a folded paper from the wallet, but she drops it as she STARTLES with Nicolas's VIBRATING cellphone on her lap. The caller is "Gabriel."

> IVY
> Gabriel? Who the hell is Gabriel?

Ivy picks it up in SPEAKER MODE, remaining quiet.

> GABRIELLA (V.O.)
> Hello? Nicolas? Are you there?

Ivy leaps to her feet as the caller is a woman.

> IVY
> No, he is not here! Who's calling?

> GABRIELLA (V.O.)
> Oh, hi! This is Gabriella.
>> (a beat)
> His wife.

Ivy's eyes well up with rage.

> GABRIELLA (V.O.)(CON'T)
> Who am I speaking to? Hello? Are you
> the receptionist? Miss, can you hear me?

IVY

Yes!

GABRIELLA (V.O.)

Oh, good. Nicolas said he would be in the
construction area all day, but I won't be
able to get to school on time today. Can
you please tell him to pick up his son?

Ivy is frozen. She tosses the cellphone into the trash. She approaches Nicolas, intending to strangle him.

IVY

You are a lying piece of shit! If your face
has never turned red in all these years,
then it will now turn blue. Dark blue!

The phone in the waste bin starts to VIBRATE. Ivy draws her hands away from Nicolas' neck, glancing at the serum bottle above the waste bin.

IVY

Yeah. Playing safe is more fun!

INT. FLOOR#2, HOSPITAL – DAY

Ivy pretends to scratch her ankle near the laboratory to check its door. It's locked. She keeps strolling, occasionally glancing at the nurses' staff ID cards. While passing by the ladies' room, she hits on an idea.

INT. LADIES' ROOM, HOSPITAL – DAY

Ivy checks both toilet stalls to make sure she is alone. She stands guard behind the door, clutching the doorknob.

INT. LOBBY, TEXTILE COMPANY – DAY

Violet and Oliver exit the elevator. Nancy is surprised.

NANCY
Mister Marlow! What are you doing
here? Oh, how is your father?

OLIVER
Fantastic! He is in a beautiful white
bed, surrounded by colorful cables!

NANCY

Excuse me?

VIOLET
He is in the hospital.
(shakes Nancy's hand)
Violet. A family friend.

NANCY
Nancy. The company secretary.

VIOLET
Pleased to meet you, Nancy.

NANCY
The pleasure is mine, thank you.

OLIVER
Oh, god, knock it off, please! Where is
she? I need to see her!

NANCY
Miss Bayley is not currently present.

OLIVER
A lie never grows old, huh, Nancy?

Oliver checks Jessica's office and the conference room. No one is in
sight. He storms back into the lobby.

NANCY
I am not lying, Mister Marlow. I mean...
Not this time.

                    OLIVER
Nancy, please! Do you have any idea
how we jumped through hoops to
get all the way down here? Look
at me! I look like a drowned rat!

Nancy looks over his awful appearance, then turns her gaze to the window. It is not pouring outside.

                    OLIVER (CON'T)
Oh, don't bother! The sky is nearly in
tears only when I'm outside without
an umbrella!
                    (imploringly)
Nancy... Please...

                    NANCY
I'm sorry, Mister Marlow, but if I tell
you where she is, it may cost me my job.

Oliver paces back and forth, ripping his hair out. Violet turns to Nancy.

                    VIOLET
And if you don't tell, it may cost them
their future.

INT. LADIES' ROOM, HOSPITAL – DAY

When a CHUBBY NURSE, 35, pushes the door to enter, Ivy pretends to be leaving quickly and bumps into her on purpose to steal her staff ID card.

                    CHUBBY NURSE
Ouch!

                    IVY
Oh, I didn't see you, sorry.

INT. FLOOR#2, HOSPITAL – DAY

Ivy heads for the laboratory, concealing the stolen ID card in her pocket.

> CHUBBY NURSE (O.S.)
> Hey, you! Hey, lady!

Ivy stops and turns around, stressed. The Chubby Nurse is staring at her from the ladies' room doorway.

> CHUBBY NURSE (CON'T)
> Next time, use the flush!

Ivy feels relieved, but she still wants to needle her.

> IVY
> Oh, so you know my urine that well,
> huh? Think twice before you judge!

The Chubby Nurse returns to the ladies' room, embarrassed.

Ivy arrives at the laboratory. She snoops around and then uses the stolen ID card to open the door.

INT. LABORATORY, HOSPITAL – DAY

Tall cabinets, medical supplies, a variety of blood and urine samples...
Ivy discovers the cabinet containing chemical bottles. Her fingers run over the labels. She smirks to herself when she finds the potassium bottle.

INT. ROOM#203, HOSPITAL – DAY

Nicolas is fast asleep. Ivy leans a chair against the door to prevent the doorknob from operating, then places a bedside table behind it to keep it stable. She then loads a syringe with potassium and injects it into Nicolas' serum cord. She draws some more and repeats the injection. The heart rate on the monitor starts to race.

INT. TAXI#3 – DAY

Behind the wheel is a BELLY DRIVER, 55. Oliver is in the backseat, gazing out the window at the people rushing around the sidewalks. Violet breaks the silence.

                    VIOLET
          I believe I owe you an apology, Oliver.
          You know, for my overreaction before.
          Like you need more trouble in your life.

                    OLIVER
          I can't judge you for having human
          values, Violet.

                    VIOLET
          Seeing you two happy together again
          will help your father's recovery for sure.

                    OLIVER
          That's what I am praying for. But first,
          I need to get through the Jessica-battle.
          I don't know what to say to her or
          where to start. The only thing I know
          for certain is that I need to devise an
          effective distraction strategy. You know,
          to keep her from becoming angry again
          the moment she sees you. I hope she
          has calmed down a little by now.

                    VIOLET
          You may consider softening things up
          with a breeze from your happy memories.

                    OLIVER
          No kind of breeze can stop this storm,
          Violet. I wish she would trust me no
          matter what. I could climb Mount Everest
          for her, yet she sent me down the rabbit
          hole. She cut me out of her life, just like
          that. It felt like a sharp slap from life.

                    VIOLET
The good news is that we can also grab
some happy surprises from life's hands.

                    OLIVER
Yeah? Like what?

                    VIOLET
For instance, I was struggling to find
a good job for months. Today I had an
interview with a well-known advertising
agency. And guess who'll be their Junior
Media Planner starting tomorrow?

                    OLIVER
Wow, I'm so happy for you, Violet! And
thanks for reminding me that the world
doesn't revolve only around me. God,
how selfish I am!

                    VIOLET
No, come on, don't say that.

                    OLIVER
Okay, tell me one more of those surprising
stories, and then I may change my mind
about hating myself.

Violet's gaze is drawn to the angel-wing accessory dangling from the
rear-view mirror.

                    VIOLET
When I was a little girl, we lived in a
small village, two hours away from
the city. Kids in our neighborhood
were often messing with me.

                    OLIVER
Why so?

> VIOLET
> Because of my father. He used to drink
> a lot and stir up trouble every other day.
> (eyes well up)
> So, my childhood was not one of the best
> ones. I used to feel so defenseless and
> lonely. Maybe that's why I've always
> wanted to have a big brother since then.
> And...

> OLIVER
> And?

> VIOLET
> And, I guess, and I hope, that he is sitting
> right next to me right now.

Oliver is deeply touched by her words. When he brotherly caresses her head, Violet's cheeks well up with tears.

> OLIVER
> You'd better believe it, you weepy young
> lady.

The Belly Driver wipes his tears away and offers Violet a tissue as well.

INT. ROOM#203, HOSPITAL – DAY

The heart rate races on the monitor.

Ivy stuffs the potassium bottle and the syringe into her purse to avoid leaving any evidence behind. Nicolas blinks awake, GROANING in pain. He feels better when he sees Ivy.

> NICOLAS
> Darling... You are here...

Ivy simply glares at him. The heart rate continues to race on the monitor. Nicolas GASPS FOR BREATH. When Ivy is about to leave the room, Nicolas barely talks again.

NICOLAS
Darling... Hold my hand...

Ivy gives him a dark stare. Nicolas GASPS FOR BREATH. Ivy notices the folded paper on the floor that she had dropped earlier. She curiously grabs it. Her eyes widen while she reads it. It's Nicolas and Gabriella's divorce decree.

IVY
Divorced? Last week? Oh, shit!

Ivy swiftly disconnects the serum cable to save him from poisoning. An engagement ring falls from Nicolas' grasp while he struggles to breathe. Ivy picks up the ring and sees that it's engraved with their names, "IVY & NICOLAS."

The heart rate on the monitor STOPS. Nicolas remains motionless in bed.

IVY
Oh, no! No, darling, please! Stay with
me! I'm begging you!

Ivy rests her ear against his chest. There's no heartbeat. Ivy performs CPR on Nicolas, crying.

INT. ROOM#401, HOSPITAL – DAY

Patrick, who is wearing an oxygen mask, TAKES a DEEP BREATH in his SLEEP and then resumes regular breathing.

INT. ROOM#203, HOSPITAL – DAY

Ivy stops doing CPR, as it's too late to bring Nicolas back. She sobs over his dead body. The door is KNOCKED.

CAREGIVER (O.S.)
Hey, what's going on in there? Open
the door!

Ivy places a kiss on Nicolas' lifeless lips. She then wears and kisses the ring. She approaches the window, climbs the windowsill, leans forward, and falls out.

The Chubby Nurse and a MALE CAREGIVER finally shoulder the door open.

> CHUBBY NURSE
> Oh, what the hell!

The Chubby Nurse checks Nicolas' pulse and realizes that he is already deceased. The Caregiver looks out the window and sees Ivy lying down on the grass in pain.

> CAREGIVER
> It's bloody hell!

EXT. BACKYARD, HOSPITAL – DAY

Ivy lies in the wet grass with broken bones. She barely sees some pigeons flying above her. They fight for the biscuits near the ceramic flowerpot on the windowsill of Room#303. As they knock the flowerpot over, it smashes Ivy's face.

The Caregiver, rushing towards Ivy, becomes frozen. Ivy dies with her eyes wide and her face covered in blood.

A sharp CLAP of THUNDER.

INT. ROOM#401, HOSPITAL – DAY

Patrick, who is wearing an oxygen mask, TAKES a DEEP BREATH in his SLEEP and then resumes regular breathing.

FLASHBACK: INT. KITCHEN, DANIEL'S APARTMENT – DAY

Sofia hangs the white rag to dry. She puts the bleach bottle back into the cabinet after closing its cap.

FLASHBACK: INT. LIVING ROOM, DANIEL'S APARTMENT – DAY

Sofia continues to knit the white scarf while watching TV.

FLASHBACK: INT. AUTO REPAIR SHOP – DAY

Daniel and the Apprentice are washing the gray car. Elliot, in a green jersey, is studying math at a table.

A car with a broken headlight pulls up near the shop. The Young Couple and their daughter Lily, who is hugging her fancy flowerpot, exit the car. Daniel greets them.

EXT. RESTAURANT STREET – DAY

Oliver and Violet exit the taxi and wave goodbye to the Belly Driver. Oliver gets upset as he accidentally steps into a puddle of mud. While shaking the mud off his cuffs, he notices a music store across the street. He motions for Violet to wait beneath an awning. Violet does so. Oliver crosses the street, causing a jam in the traffic, and he finally rushes into the music store.

INT. ROOM#401, HOSPITAL – DAY

Patrick blinks awake. He slowly removes his oxygen mask. Doctor Francisco enters the room.

> DOCTOR FRANCISCO
> Beauty sleep is over, huh? How are you
> feeling now?

> PATRICK
> I'm not sure. Kind of relieved, I suppose.
> Where is my son, Frankie?

> DOCTOR FRANCISCO
> No idea. He must still be there wherever
> you sent him to.

As Patrick can't breathe sufficiently, the Doctor places the oxygen mask back on. Nurse Andrea shows up.

> NURSE ANDREA
> Excuse me, Doctor Francisco. I have something to tell you. Could you come outside? Please?

The Doctor nods, then turns to Patrick.

> DOCTOR FRANCISCO
> I feel like a tennis ball in the shape of a human body.

The Doctor exits. Patrick can see Nurse Andrea and Doctor Francisco talking about something serious through the glass wall, but he is unable to hear them.

INT. INTENSIVE CARE UNIT HALLWAY, HOSPITAL – DAY

Nurse Andrea and Doctor Francisco discuss the incident.

> DOCTOR FRANCISCO
> My god... This hospital has gotten out of hand.

> NURSE ANDREA
> I know, Doctor! Murder and suicide at once!

> DOCTOR FRANCISCO
> No need to announce it all the way to Manchester, Andrea.

> NURSE ANDREA
> (lowers her voice)
> Sorry. Here is the ID card of the deceased girl. Ivy Selton.

Doctor Francisco examines the ID card.

                    DOCTOR FRANCISCO
          She was only twenty-two, huh?

                     NURSE ANDREA
          We quickly checked her data. Her name
          had been registered as a donor four years
          ago. It's AB-positive.

                    DOCTOR FRANCISCO
          Well, it's worth a shot. Tell the guys to
          start analyzing. We are already out of time.

Nurse Andrea rushes down the stairs. POLICE SIRENS can be HEARD.

EXT. RESTAURANT STREET – DAY

Oliver emerges from the music store, happily holding a CD. Violet,
across the street, enthusiastically applauds. Oliver crosses the street
and approaches the restaurant's entrance. A well-dressed DOORMAN,
50, steps in his way, assuming Oliver is homeless.

                       DOORMAN
          I don't have any change, pal! Move along!

Oliver becomes puzzled. He notices his awful appearance reflected in
the glass door.

                        OLIVER
          Oh, no, no, you got me wrong!

                       DOORMAN
          I guess you got the address wrong, pal!
          Come on, get lost!

                        OLIVER
          Look, "pal"! I'm at the right place, and
          I didn't have time to stop by a beauty
          salon, okay? So, please stay out of my
          way! I'm in a life-or-death situation!

                    DOORMAN
          Not yet, but you will be in a minute if
          you keep jabbering here!

As Violet approaches the entrance door, the Doorman steps aside to let her in.

                    DOORMAN
          Good afternoon, Miss. Enjoy your lunch.

                    VIOLET
          Thank you, sir. However, I only have a
          hunger for peace today.

The Doorman looks at her blankly. Violet whispers in Oliver's ear and takes the CD from him. Oliver seems puzzled at first, but then he smiles.

                    OLIVER
          Okay then, number one!

Violet agrees with a nod. Oliver dashes down the street. Violet turns to the Doorman.

                    VIOLET
          Sir, could you do me a simple favor?
          It won't cost you a dime, I promise.

INT. ELEGANT RESTAURANT – DAY

Italians, Arthur, and Jessica, in a black dress, are at the end of their lunch. Waiters show up to clear the table. Jessica tries to finish her tiny piece of chocolate souffle even the waiter removes her plate. Jessica finally leaves the spoon to let him go. She realizes that the table smiles at her.

                    JESSICA
          It was my favorite dessert.

The song "A Thousand Stars" suddenly fills the restaurant. Jessica becomes surprised.

JESSICA
Gosh, I can't believe this.

SERGIO
Let me guess, Jessica. This song is also
one of your favorites?

JESSICA
Well, it used to be, Sergio.

Jessica sadly touches the ring mark on her finger. Fabio notices Oliver
trying to walk along the windowsill.

FABIO
Mamma Mia! Isn't that Oliver?

JESSICA
Yes, Fabio. He proposed to me through
this song, but how did you know?

FABIO
No, I mean, I'd only seen him once, but
I think that's him out there, climbing
up the window!

Jessica becomes puzzled when she sees Oliver struggling to maintain
his balance on the windowsill. He looks at Jessica lovingly while singing
along with "Billy Fury."

OLIVER
"A thousand stars in the skies... Like
the stars in your eyes..."

JESSICA
Oh, good God!

Jessica immediately opens the window. Oliver jumps inside and
attempts to dance with her. Waiters arrive to get rid of him. Marco tries
to lighten the mood.

MARCO
That's alright, guys! The gentleman is
our guest of honor. You can go. *Grazie*!

JESSICA
(embarrassed)
So sorry...

Waiters bow half-respectful and half- displeased, then they return to their work. Jessica gets rid of Oliver's hands, speaking in a low voice.

JESSICA
What the hell are you doing here, looking
like a drowned rat?

However, she is heard by the table.

ROMINA
Seems like he is serenading for love and
peace. How cute!

ARTHUR
Very creative, Oliver! Well done!

The table APPLAUDS Oliver while Marco barely smiles.

OLIVER
Thanks, guys! It's great to see you all
again! Please accept my apologies for
the interruption, as well as my untidy
appearance.
(grabs Jessica's hand)
But I need to steal her for a moment.

MARCO
What's meant to be will be, Oliver.

Jessica walks away with Oliver, only to avoid another awkward scene.

JESSICA
Are you out of your mind?

OLIVER
For a while now!

Oliver points at Violet, who is talking to a YOUNG WAITER near the entrance door.

OLIVER
Someone is waiting for you to explain
how I became an innocent victim.

JESSICA
Gosh, on top of that, you've brought
her down here? You are a discourteous,
wet rat with no shame! Unbelievable!

OLIVER
It's good that you only met dry and
humble ones! Just keep walking.

Meanwhile, Arthur and the Italians converse.

SERGIO
Wow, she managed to give a great
presentation today. Despite her
personal issues, I mean.

ROMINA
Esatto, Sergio! She must have been
devastated the whole day.

FABIO
She is an absolute pro!

ARTHUR
What can I say, Fabio? She is!

ROMINA
I hope they kiss and make up.

                    ARTHUR
          I hope so, too, Romina. Otherwise, she
          might even eat us with her souffle at
          dinner tonight!

While the table LAUGHS, Marco sips his wine.

                    MARCO
          Well, I'm sure that we'll have many
          more great deals with these brilliant
          and responsible friends for a long
          long time. And we absolutely loved
          their new project. Right, folks?

His coworkers confirm with a nod. Arthur is surprised.

                    ARTHUR
          Wow, I'll drink to that!

They raise their wine glasses. Marco finishes his wine in one gulp.

                    MARCO
          Okay, folks. Since we have completed
          the biggest part of our work here, we
          can have our dinner on the plane tonight.

At a table near the entrance door, Violet tells Jessica the entire story.
Oliver nervously paces back and forth.

                    VIOLET
          This is exactly what happened, Jessica.
          I tried to explain it to you yesterday,
          but you were pretty angry. For a good
          reason, of course. And the dog I mentioned
          was in my arms, if you remember.
          I am deeply sorry for everything.

                    JESSICA
          No, Violet, I am the one who's sorry.
          Gosh, you must've thought that I was
          a dreadful witch.

> VIOLET
>
> No, I just thought that you were a woman
> in love.

> OLIVER
>
> Same difference!

The two women turn to Oliver. Oliver looks at Jessica.

> OLIVER
>
> So, babe, do you believe me now?

> JESSICA
>
> Oh, my gosh! So your father was really
> mugged?

> OLIVER
>
> And attacked.

EXT. RESTAURANT STREET – DAY

It's lightly raining. Violet, Oliver, and Jessica emerge from the restaurant, trying to fit under Jessica's pink umbrella. Violet gratefully shakes the Doorman's hand. Oliver answers his RINGING cellphone.

> OLIVER
>
> Doc, I need good news! What? Seriously?
> You are my hero, Doc! Yeah, we are on
> our way!

Oliver shares the news with the two women.

> OLIVER
>
> We did it, ladies! We now have a lovely
> second-hand kidney!

The three share hugs. The Young Waiter emerges from the restaurant, holding a pair of shoes and an ironed white shirt. He approaches Oliver.

                    YOUNG WAITER
          Excuse me, sir. I don't mean to be
          disrespectful, but I heard your story,
          and I thought you might want to greet
          your father with a better appearance.

A surprised Oliver looks at the two women first and then hugs the
Young Waiter.

INT. OPERATING THEATRE – DAY

Patrick is on the operating table. Doctor Francisco, in a surgical gown,
steps in. The two exchange a meaningful smile. Doctor confirms the
ANESTHETIST with a nod. The Anesthetist starts the process. Patrick's
eyes slowly close. Doctor asks for a surgical instrument.

                    DOCTOR FRANCISCO
          Scalpel!

The Surgical Nurse hands him a silver-gray scalpel.

- INSERT FLASHBACK -

A silver-gray jackknife is in his hand while the First Burglar rounds the
corner of ALLEY#2. He tosses it into a waste container, then pulls the
deposit bag from beneath his coat and hides it under the container.

While casually walking away, he sees the two cops running after him.
He gestures, "What's the problem?" and calmly raises his hands. A cop
frisks him but finds nothing suspicious. He then removes his ski mask.
We see that the First Burglar is Charles.

- END FLASHBACK -

Patrick's surgery is ongoing.

                    DOCTOR FRANCISCO
          Hook!

The Surgical Nurse hands him a skin hook.

- INSERT FLASHBACK -

The tattoo shaped like a hook on his neck comes in sight, when the Second Burglar leaps onto the bus at the last moment and removes his ski mask. We see that the Second Burglar is Hector.

- END FLASHBACK -

Patrick's surgery is ongoing.

                    DOCTOR FRANCISCO
          Elevator!

The Surgical Nurse hands him a skin surgical elevator.

- INSERT FLASHBACK -

As they remove their ski masks while hiding in a vintage elevator, we see that the Third Burglar is Nicolas, and the Forth Burglar is Ivy.

- END FLASHBACK -

With each passing minute, the surgery becomes more and more stressful. A nurse wipes the sweat from Doctor Francisco's brow.

INT. ENTRANCE LOBBY, HOSPITAL – DAY

Bryan flips through a hospital magazine. He likes a photo of a happy family with a young woman holding a bunch of grapes for her husband and son. Violet, Oliver, and Jessica arrive at the hospital. Oliver now has a much better appearance. Bryan jumps to his feet.

                    BRYAN
          Hey, boss! They've already taken him
          to the surgery room!

                    OLIVER
          I know, Bryan, but you didn't have to
          drive all the way down here, I told you.

                    BRYAN
          Come on, boss! Just tell me if there's
          anything I can do to help.

                    JESSICA
          Pray, Bryan. Just pray.

Oliver wraps his arm around Jessica and kisses her on the brow. He then looks over at Violet and Bryan.

                    OLIVER
          You guys haven't met yet, right? Violet,
          this is Bryan. He is my right hand. And
          this is Violet. She is... Well, she is my
          sister, from another father and mother.

Violet feels grateful for his description. Bryan and Violet exchange candid handshakes.

EXT. ALLEY#2 – NIGHT

Bulldozer and Liam, in their coveralls, pull a waste container toward the garbage truck. A bank deposit bag appears on the ground. Bulldozer becomes surprised when he sees the label that reads, "MR. PATRICK MARLOW."

INT. KITCHEN, BASEMENT APARTMENT – NIGHT

Nobody is home. Blackflies are buzzing around the BEER BOTTLE that used to belong to Hector.

INT. BATHROOM, BASEMENT APARTMENT – NIGHT

The tap is dripping. There is a COMB by the sink that used to belong to Nicolas.

INT. LIVING ROOM, BASEMENT APARTMENT – NIGHT

There are a PAIR of BLACK GLOVES, a BLACK SKI MASK, and a cigarette on the table that used to belong to Charles.

INT. FOYER, BASEMENT APARTMENT – NIGHT

A swarm of cockroaches are crawling around the RED BOOTS that used to belong to Ivy.

INT. WAITING LOUNGE, HOSPITAL – NIGHT

Violet and Jessica are seated on a bench, waiting for good news. Bryan and Oliver are conversing by the large window.

> BRYAN
> I almost forgot, boss. Before I came here,
> I got a call from the glazier. He said that
> something had happened to the frosted
> glass we had ordered for your office door.

> OLIVER
> I couldn't care less about that door right
> now, Bryan.

> BRYAN
> But he also said that they would perfectly
> glaze a new one and deliver it first thing
> in the morning, and completely for free.
> I mean, as a gift.

> OLIVER
> As a gift? Why so?

> BRYAN
> No idea, boss. Strange, right?

Bulldozer and Miguel appear down the hallway and rush towards them, out of breath. Oliver becomes surprised.

OLIVER
Bulldozer?

MIGUEL
Oliver, look what he's got here!
He found Señor's stolen money!

OLIVER
What?

Bulldozer hands Oliver the deposit bag. Oliver is speechless.

BULLDOZER
It was hidden under a waste container.
It's little wet, but I hope it's still fine.

JESSICA
This is unbelievable.

VIOLET
It' almost like a boomerang.

BRYAN
Yeah, a rectangular one.

BULLDOZER
Mrs. Howard was telling everyone
about the incident today. So, I was
surprised when I found this bag with
your father's name on it, and I wanted
to hand it over to you right away.

OLIVER
(thankfully hugs Bulldozer)
God bless you, man!

MIGUEL
Any news about him yet?

JESSICA
Still in surgery.

BULLDOZER
Well, I have to return to clean up the city.
People never take a day off from littering,
you know.

MIGUEL
Yeah, and I have to give him a ride.
We'll keep our fingers crossed for Señor!

OLIVER
You guys are the best! Thanks!

Miguel and Bulldozer rush down the stairs. Bryan's cellphone RINGS.
He walks away while talking.

BRYAN
Hello? No, we are still waiting...

Oliver seems upset, looking at the bank bag on his lap. Jessica strokes
his back, then glances at her watch.

JESSICA
Oh, honey, may I borrow your cellphone
for a minute? I need to call my mom
to see if they could catch the flight.

OLIVER
Sure, babe, take it.

Oliver hands her his cellphone.

JESSICA
By the way, I assure you that I won't
peek into your inbox or anything.

OLIVER
Be my guest.

JESSICA
I'd rather be your wife, hon.

Jessica drops a kiss on Oliver's lips, and then she makes a call, walking away.

Violet is standing by the large window; her gaze fixed on the clock tower across the street. It reads 5:05 a.m. Oliver approaches her.

                    OLIVER
          A penny for your thoughts?

                    VIOLET
          I was just wondering how our lives
          would have shaped today if I had
          acted more conscious yesterday.

The tower clock runs backwards at high speed, and we JOURNEY BACK to the PARALLEL UNIVERSE...

FLASHBACK: INT. LIVING ROOM, BASEMENT APARTMENT – DAY

Nicolas and Hector play cards on the sofa. Charles arrives and throws his keys on the table, exhausted.

                    HECTOR
          Hey, lost friend! You finally found
          your way back home, huh?

                    CHARLES
          Cut it short, man!

                    NICOLAS
          Hey, Charles, I've successfully passed
          the patience test you imposed on me.
          Don't you think?

Charles tosses a ring pouch at him. Nicolas catches it in the air and checks the golden ring. It's engraved with the names "IVY & NICOLAS."

                    NICOLAS (CON'T)
          Wow, this is far beyond my expectations!
          Thanks, man!

Charles sits at the table and exhales.

                        HECTOR
What's wrong with you today, man?

                        CHARLES
I'm just tired. And not from a stupid
card game.

                        HECTOR
But from pretending to be a wealthy
deaf-mute, I guess.

Hector LAUGHS, but then stops because no one else is laughing. Charles turns to Nicolas.

                        CHARLES
So, what's your plan? Hector and I can
disappear if you propose to her tonight?

Nicolas reflexively throws some playing cards towards Charles, speaking in a low voice.

                        NICOLAS
Tone it down a notch, man. Ivy is in
the shower. She may hear you. I will
make my proposal tomorrow evening,
after finishing the job. Tomorrow is
our third dating anniversary, you know.

Hector collects the strewn cards.

                        CHARLES
You are an incurable romantic, man!
By the way, guys, we won't be working
tomorrow.

                        NICOLAS
What? Why?

HECTOR
But it's the "throwing eggs at windshields
day!" My favorite!

Hector dons his ski mask just to make a funny scene.

NICOLAS
No, bro, it's Monday tomorrow. It's the
"bank jugging day."

HECTOR
Oh, right! I forgot.

CHARLES
It doesn't matter at all, guys. We are
calling it off. I'll have other things to
be done tomorrow.

NICOLAS
What could be so damn important as
to cripple our schedule?
            (suspicious)
Or you have a date or something?

Hector removes his ski mask, captivated by the subject. Charles just
pretends to take a deep puff on his unlit cigarette. Nicolas throws some
more playing cards at him.

NICOLAS (CON'T)
Oh, man, you do have a date! Who is she?
Come on, tell us!

CHARLES
Calm down, Nicolas, it's not a date, okay?
I'll just drive her to a job interview. That's
all.

HECTOR
Huh! When did you start doing favors for
others?

NICOLAS
Bro, he just stole a ring for me! And it's
engraved with our names! I'm not even
gonna ask how he did this!

HECTOR
Oh, right, the ring... I forgot.
(to Charles)
Thank you, man!

NICOLAS
It seems like your memory is furiously
getting old, bro!

Hector throws some playing cards at Nicolas.

HECTOR
That's bull! You look at yourself! You're
the one who forgot Gabriella's birthday
last month!

Ivy, in her bathrobe, steps into the room.

IVY (CON'T)
Gabriella? Who the hell is Gabriella?

Nicolas and Hector are baffled. Charles heaves a sigh.

CHARLES
Nicolas, I believe the time has come.

IVY
Time has come for what? What the hell
is going on here? Who is Gabriella?

NICOLAS
Darling...

Nicolas tries to hug her, but Ivy beats him with a towel.

> IVY
> Do not ever call me that! Who the hell
> is Gabriella? Answer me! Answer me!

Charles motions to Hector, meaning "Let's vanish," and the two leave the apartment. Ivy slaps Nicolas with the towel.

> NICOLAS
> Please, darling, I'll tell you everything
> if you lower your weapon right now!

Ivy angrily hits Nicolas one last time.

FLASHBACK: EXT. BLIND ALLEY – DUSK

Charles and Hector emerge from an old apartment building and stroll down the alley. Charles pretends to take a deep puff on his unlit cigarette. He then thinks that it's a stupid idea and simply tosses it towards the lilac tree.

> HECTOR
> That mystery girl impressed you big
> time, I guess, huh?

> CHARLES
> I guess so, too, man!

As the night falls, the apartments that surround the alley begin to light up one by one.

FLASHBACK: INT. LIVING ROOM, BASEMENT APARTMENT – NIGHT

Nicolas tells Ivy the entire story.

> NICOLAS
> I swear that Gabriella and I were
> never in love. We were both very
> young and barely knew each other.
> My parents forced me to marry her.

                    IVY
Bullshit!

                  NICOLAS
It's true. Because, I used to be a little
handful, you know. Anyway, we tried
but couldn't make it work, and we
ended up as two good friends.

                    IVY
Friends? You said you had a son!
You have a child with her!

                  NICOLAS
Even his presence couldn't save the
marriage. My little Benji. He is ten
now. He and his mother think that
I am a construction worker who is
obliged to work mostly out of town.

                    IVY
What? No way.

                  NICOLAS
Yes, darling. As you can see, I've kind of
chosen to see my son less to see you more.

                    IVY
Are you expecting an award for this?

                  NICOLAS
I've already been rewarded with the
past three years. Three awesome years
with you.

Ivy is not sure if he is telling the truth.

                  NICOLAS (CON'T)
So, I assured Gabriella that everything
would work for the best for our son
and finally convinced her to divorce.

                    IVY
          You know what? You are nothing but
          a compulsive liar!

Nicolas pulls the folded divorce decree from his wallet.

                    NICOLAS
          Here is the official document. We
          divorced last week.

Ivy is speechless. Nicolas grabs her hand and tries to put the ring on
her finger while looking at Ivy in the eye.

                    NICOLAS (CON'T)
          You are my other half, darling.

                    IVY
              (withdraws her hand)
          Ouch! Are you planning to smash my
          finger like you did with my heart?

Nicolas innocently holds up the engagement ring.

                    NICOLAS
          Actually, I was planning to do something
          better, but I guess making surprises isn't
          my thing.
              (kneels in front of her)
          My sweet angel, will you marry me?

                    IVY
          Holy shit!

                    NICOLAS
          I believe that it's a "Yes."

                    IVY
          You know me too well!

Ivy leaps into his arms. Nicolas gently places the ring on her finger. Ivy
kisses the ring.

IVY (CON'T)
From now on, you will always be
honest with me, okay? About
everything. Do not ever make
me turn into the Angel of Death.

NICOLAS
Deal!

They kiss passionately.

FLASH FORWARD: INT. BOWLING ALLEY – DAY

Violet and Charles go bowling. Violet bowls a strike, and the game ends. She has a greater score than him.

VIOLET
Hey, I beat you!

CHARLES
I'm afraid you did.

VIOLET
So, are you giving up?

CHARLES
No, never.

VIOLET
Then nobody can ever call you a "loser."

Violet smiles and hands him a bowling ball. They start a new game. Charles bowls a strike.

FLASH FORWARD: INT. KITCHEN, BASEMENT APARTMENT –NIGHT

Nicolas and Hector are eating pasta at a sloppy dinner table. Ivy seems upset, playing with her meal.

                    IVY
Can someone tell me what the hell
is going on with Charles? His
sluggishness is driving me insane!
When are we gonna get back to work,
huh? It's been almost two months!

                    NICOLAS
He probably doesn't want to jeopardize
his relationship with that sociologist girl.

                    HECTOR
Yeah. I bet he is already in love with her.

                    IVY
So, can someone serve their precious
love on my plate? Cause I can't keep
eating pasta anymore!

Ivy tosses her fork onto the table and paces around.

                    HECTOR
But I serve it with a different sauce
every other day. I am hurt.

                    NICOLAS
Darling, please, come sit here.

                    IVY
More than seventy brand new
smartphones are sleeping in his
rusty trunk! What is he waiting for
to monetize them, huh? To find us
gnawing on these chairs and walls?

                    HECTOR
Charles already said that we wouldn't
turn them in for cash.

IVY
What? Tell me you are joking!
     (to Nicolas)
Tell me he is joking!

NICOLAS
He was mumbling something about
giving them away to the poor.

IVY
To the poor? Oh, right, because we
are living in a huge castle! Man, I'll
choke him to death! I swear I will!

NICOLAS
Darling, please calm down.

IVY
You calm down!

HECTOR
He was also talking about some other
job the other day.

IVY
Finally, some good news! I hope it's
not another bank jugging. I want to
try different things.

HECTOR
It's different, Ivy. Because he said
"legitimate business."

IVY
Legitimate?

HECTOR
Yeah, you know, like selling sandwiches
or something.

                    IVY
What? No way! If I wanted to be a
sissy girl, I wouldn't have abandoned
home in the first place!

                    NICOLAS
Darling, don't get angry with Charles.
You know well that we all owe him big.

                    HECTOR
Yeah. Thanks to his super brain, we are
still surviving with no criminal record.

Hector and Nicolas exchange winks.

                    HECTOR – NICOLAS
Playing safe is more fun!

                    IVY
That's bullshit!

                    NICOLAS
Darling, stop acting like a child and sit
here. Hunger puts more pressure on
your nerves.

Nicolas refills Ivy's glass. Ivy stops pacing and glances at the water jug.
She barely smirks. Nicolas notices.

                    NICOLAS (CON'T)
And do not ever think about doing
something stupid on your own, okay?
Never ever.

Ivy simply sits down and kisses Nicolas. Nicolas feeds her pasta. Hector
regains his happiness.

FLASH FORWARD: INT. KITCHEN, OLD LADY'S FLAT – DAY

A REPAIRMAN, 30, is working on a clogged sink. The Hunchback Old Lady appears in the doorway, clutching a watering can.

> HUNCHBACK OLD LADY
> How is it going, boy?

> REPAIRMAN
> The hard part is over, ma'am. Give me
> five more minutes.

> HUNCHBACK OLD LADY
> Oh, beautiful! Then you can taste my
> famous mint tea in six minutes.

FLASH FORWARD: INT. LIVING ROOM, OLD LADY'S FLAT – DAY

The Hunchback Old Lady waters the potted mint plants arranged on the outside of the windowsill, half-singing.

FLASH FORWARD: INT. OLD LADY'S BUILDING – DAY

Ivy places her ear on the Hunchback Old Lady's apartment door and can barely hear her SINGING. She snoops around and starts pouring a bucket of water underneath the door.

FLASH FORWARD: INT. LIVING ROOM, OLD LADY'S FLAT – DAY

The Hunchback Old Lady notices some water flowing in through the doorsill.

> HUNCHBACK OLD LADY
> Oh, my… What is that?

Just as she curiously opens the door, Ivy grabs her neck with her arm and closes her mouth.

                    IVY
          Show me where you hid your jewels,
          or I'll show you the color of your
          fusty blood!

The Hunchback Old Lady gets scared and points to a vintage cabinet near the window. Ivy drags her there, then pushes her down and searches through the drawers. The Hunchback Old Lady coughs and barely shouts.

                    HUNCHBACK OLD LADY
          Help! Please, help me...

                    IVY
          Who are you talking to, you wrinkled
          moron? I know that you live here all
          alone! So, shut up!

The Repairman emerges from the kitchen.

                    REPAIRMAN
          Hey, what's going on here?

A puzzled Ivy takes out a silver-gray jackknife.

                    IVY
          Stay away or I'll kill--

The Repairman pulls away the long rug, causing Ivy on the other end to lose her balance and fall out the window. The Repairman and the Hunchback Old Lady look out the window. Ivy is writhing in agony on the sidewalk among the broken flowerpots.

MOOD MUSIC begins in the BACKGROUND.

FLASH FORWARD: EXT. HYDE PARK – DAY

Hector, Nicolas, Ivy, and Charles are now street vendors. Hector prepares the avocado sandwiches. Nicolas and his son, BENJI, 12, assist him with peeling avocados.

Violet is seated under a plane tree, designing a flyer to introduce their sandwiches to the neighborhood.

Ivy, who is paralyzed from the neck down, is confined to a wheelchair. She observes Violet's white-hope drawings.

Charles brings Hector a large bag of avocados. He then sits next to Violet and admires her drawings.

FLASH FORWARD: INT. CHARLES' SELF-SERVICE DINER - DAY

Hector prepares meals in the open kitchen. Charles places them on the glass display counter. An eight-month-pregnant Violet is behind the cash register. Charles, her husband, brings her a glass of lemonade and kisses her. They are deeply in love.

Ivy is in a wheelchair. Nicolas plays cards with her, as well as on her behalf.

After finishing her meal, a FEMALE CUSTOMER buys a yellow philanthropy card from Violet and puts it in the basket hanging on the wall.

A HOMELESS MAN takes a yellow card from the basket and hands it to Charles. Charles hands him a sandwich. The Homeless Man gratefully bows and exits the diner while eating his tasty sandwich.

FLASH FORWARD: INT. CHARLES' RESTAURANT – DAY

Hector and his two assistants cook in the back kitchen. The dishes are served by waiters.

A 5-month-pregnant Violet greets customers in the doorway. Charles is working behind the cash register. He hands his TWO-YEAR-OLD SON a green philanthropy card and makes him place it in the fancy basket hanging on the wall. Violet places a few grapes in the mouths of Charles and her son. They both kiss Violet on the cheeks.

Ivy is confined to a wheelchair. Nicolas feeds her soup. As it dribbles down, Nicolas gently wipes Ivy's chin and then kisses her on the brow.

FLASH FORWARD: EXT. HYDE PARK – DAY

A beautiful summer day. Oliver, Jessica, and their FIVE- YEAR-OLD TWIN DAUGHTERS are having a good time. Patrick hands a couple of pink balloons to his granddaughters before hurrying into the public restroom.

Charles and Violet are seated on a bench. Their FOUR-YEAR- OLD SON and TWO-YEAR-OLD DAUGHTER enjoy running around.

Eventually, the four kids begin to play together on the playground. Their parents great each other, shake hands, and begin to chat.

Patrick returns with two more balloons, one pink and one blue, and hands them to Charles and Violet's kids.

Ivy is in a wheelchair under a plane tree. Nicolas reads her the book "AD 2150" by Thea Alexander.

Hector lies on the grass, listening to music. The BACKGROUND MUSIC STOPS as he presses the STOP button on his MP3 player.

INT. WAITING LOUNGE, HOSPITAL – NIGHT

The headlight of an ambulance REFLECTS OFF the window, and we return from the PARALLEL UNIVERSE. Violet and Oliver are staring at the clock tower. It reads 5:05 a.m.

OLIVER
Yeah, who knows what could happen?

Jessica rushes down the stairwell towards them.

JESSICA
Honey! Honey, I just saw Doctor
Francisco! The surgery is over!

                    OLIVER
So, can I see my father? Is he okay?

                    JESSICA
I think he's still unconscious. But the
doctor said he was a "good old son of
a gun," whatever that means.

                    OLIVER
I think it means something good, right?

                    JESSICA
We can confirm it with the Doctor, hon.
He is already in his office, waiting for us.

Jessica and Oliver rush upstairs. Violet sits on a bench. Bryan walks
down the stairs with two paper cups of coffee.

                    VIOLET
Bryan, the surgery is over! Mister
Marlow has nailed it!

                    BRYAN
Yes, I know. I just saw the boss on the
way. Great news, huh? Some coffee?

                    VIOLET
Oh, very kind of you. Thanks.

Violet takes a sip. Bryan sits next to her and offers her creamer and
sugar packs.

                    BRYAN
Not sure how you like it.

                    VIOLET
It's perfect the way it is. Thank you,
Bryan.

                    BRYAN
My pleasure.

Bryan puts some sugar into his coffee.

> BRYAN (CON'T)
> What a day, huh?

> VIOLET
> It was full of compelling moments.

> BRYAN
> That's an interesting description.

> VIOLET
> Yet it's correct. Anyway. Tomorrow
> will be a much better day for all of us.

> BRYAN
> I wouldn't count on it, Violet. There
> are a lot more bad people in this world,
> and you never know when you'll run
> into one of them.

> VIOLET
> Actually, there is no such thing as "bad
> people."

> BRYAN
> Excuse me? So, your home is on another
> planet, I guess.

> VIOLET
> No, we share the same address, don't
> worry. It's just... It's hard to categorize
> people as a 100% good or 100% percent
> bad. After all, everyone must have left
> some footprints on both of those paths.

> BRYAN
> Well, I don't know whose feet are where,
> but I am absolutely certain that I am
> a good person, Violet. And you don't
> seem like a witch on a broom, either.

VIOLET
Thank you, Bryan, but that's already
the point. For instance, a sweet-looking
delivery guy who secretly spits on your
pizza may be considered as a good person
in his neighborhood. The same goes for
the line-jumper housewife in the supermarket.
Or... Or a girl who pretends to be pregnant
to trick taxi drivers. I mean, can't you
just see it, Bryan? It's on everyone's
lips. Easy to say, but hard to prove.

BRYAN
Wait, are you trying to tell me that even
I might do some bad things to some
people? Because I can assure you that
there's no such world, Violet.

VIOLET
But the game is still on. So, none of us
can be totally sure that we will never
rob, kill, or injure someone. We all have
the potential to do those things, hiding
somewhere within us.

BRYAN
Sorry, but I've never felt any of those sick
potentials within me, okay? And I'm almost
thirty.

Bryan sips his coffee in one gulp, as if it were vodka.

VIOLET
Then maybe the maturity level of your
soul is high enough to tame those human
instincts. Or, maybe nothing or no one
has stimulated you enough to release
them by now.

BRYAN
That sounds a little scary. Don't you think?

Violet simply shrugs. She looks up at the bright stars in the dark sky, noticeable through the large window.

                    VIOLET
          Not seeing the sun at night doesn't
          change the fact that it's still there
          in flames. That's all I'm saying.

                    BRYAN
          Okay, Violet, well said. But, with all
          due respect, I can't say that I agree
          with you. There is no doubt that many
          people are still being hurt outside
          right now. Do you know why?

                    VIOLET
          Why?

                    BRYAN
          Because there are bad people. One
          hundred percent bad.

Bryan crumples his coffee cup and tosses it into the waste bin.

                    VIOLET
          But "bad" for whom?

                    BRYAN
          What's that supposed to mean now?

                    VIOLET
          The view you see can be changed depending
          on the window you are standing at.

                    BRYAN
          Not always. Some things in life are crystal
          clear, Violet. You are either good or bad.
          End of story.

Bryan feels warm. He takes off his jacket and rolls up the sleeves of his shirt. Violet sips her coffee.

VIOLET
Okay. How about this story? Let's say a very sad man comes home with a brand new big-screen TV to cheer up his ill wife, who's been bedridden for months. Would you describe him as a "bad guy?"

BRYAN
Of course not. Who could say that?

VIOLET
No? Okay. So then let's say you see a man breaking into a store to steal a big-screen TV and punching the people who try to stop him. Would you describe him as a "bad guy?"

BRYAN
Of course, I would!

VIOLET
So, what if it's the same guy in both stories? You are now in conflict with yourself, right?

BRYAN
So, how are we going to call that guy?

VIOLET
"Lost". I mean, it is up to us to choose which path we'll take in life, but if we keep jumping between those two paths, we are most likely to become lost.

BRYAN
Then let me tell you that eighty percent of the people on this planet are "lost!"

VIOLET
Well, I'm not quite sure about that
percentage, Bryan.
          (sips her coffee)
I remember once, when I was four or
five years old, I was happily running
around in the forest, eating my chocolate
bar, and chasing a colorful butterfly,
completely unaware that I was heading
for a dreadful cliff.

BRYAN
Oh, no... Then what happened?

VIOLET
Well, until my parents found me near
the cliff edge, I just kept running,
laughing, and clapping my hands, with
my head in the clouds. Do you know why?

BRYAN
Why?

VIOLET
Because I had no idea that I was lost.

Bryan nods, even if he is still trying to understand what she means. He
wipes the sweat from his brow with his sleeve. Violet notices the scar
on his wrist.

VIOLET
Oh, what happened to your wrist?
Seems like a deep one.

BRYAN
Oh, you mean, this scar? It's nothing.
Just an unpleasant memory from my
college days.

VIOLET
Fighting?

BRYAN
No, no. The case was about my ex-girlfriend.
A cheating and unpredictable girlfriend.

VIOLET
Oh, shoot! Did she do this to you?

BRYAN
No... I did.
            (off her puzzled look)
Okay, I am not proud of it, but I was filled
with rage on the day I found out the ugly
truth. The pain doesn't have to always be
physical. It can also be emotional, right?
And I'm not sure which one is the worst.
God... On that weekend, I really wanted
to punish them both! But instead...

Bryan glances at his scar once more, then covers his face in disappointment.

BRYAN
Oh, God! Now you'll say that I've
already injured someone, right? Myself!

Violet sighs sadly, then finishes her coffee. Bryan watches her gently throw her coffee cup into the waste bin.

BRYAN (CON'T)
You are an interesting girl, I need to say.

VIOLET
I am just a girl who tends to question life.

BRYAN
So, have you discovered any remarkable
results?

VIOLET
So far, just one.

INT. HOSPITAL ROOM – NIGHT

The room is decorated with colorful balloons. The bank bag sits on the nightstand. There is a framed JING&JANG picture on the wall.

> VIOLET (V.O.)(CON'T)
> There is no such thing as "pure evil" or
> "pure angel."

Patrick is seated in his bed, seems peaceful with his hands are held by Oliver and Jessica. Patrick brings their hands together on his chest. The three share a warm smile.

> VIOLET (V.O.)(CON'T)
> There are just options… and choices…

The song, "King for Tonight" performed by Billy Fury, BEGINS in the BACKGROUND.

Oliver goes to Jessica, kneels in front of her, and puts the engagement ring back on her finger. They kiss and embrace each other.

Jessica inhales deeply, as if she needs to boost her courage, then pulls an ultrasound photo from a lilac envelope and happily displays it. She is two months pregnant with twins. Oliver embraces her with great happiness. He admires the photo and hands it to Patrick.

Patrick tears up as he sees the very first photo of his grandkids. He places it on his chest. Jessica wipes Patrick's tears away with a lilac handkerchief.

Doctor Francisco steps in. Oliver gives him a warm hug, gesturing that they are expecting twins. The Doctor hugs them all and heartily congratulates them. Nurse Andrea rushes inside because he needs Doctor Francisco, so he is dragged out of the room by her.
Oliver and Jessica dance around. Patrick uses the lilac handkerchief to wipe away his happy tears.

FADE OUT.

www.ingramcontent.com/pod-product-compliance
Lightning Source LLC
Chambersburg PA
CBHW031255060726
47590CB00003B/913